Ai POISON

DRAGON DESCENDANTS
Book 2

FROM
USA TODAY BESTSELLING AUTHOR
J.L WEIL

MW00884096

CONTENTS

COPYRIGHTS

Edited by Allisyn Ma.
Proofread by Stephany Wallace
Cover Design by Alerim. All Rights Reserved.
Interior Design and Formatting by Stephany Wallace. All Rights Reserved.

A Dark Magick Publishing publication, Dec 2018
www.jlweil.com

DRAGON DESCENDANTS

A REVERSE HAREM SERIES

WRITTEN BY J.L. WEIL

The Raven Series
White Raven, book1
Black Crow, book2
Soul Symmetry, book3

The Divisa Series
Saving Angel, book1.
Hunting Angel, book2.
Chasing Angel, book3.
Loving Angel, book4.
Redeeming Angel, book5.
Losing Emma, A Divisa Novella
Breaking Emma, A Divisa Novella

Luminescence Trilogy
Luminescence, book1
Amethyst Tears, book2
Moondust, book3
Darkmist, A Luminescenece Novella, book4

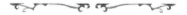

DRAGON DESCENDANTS

A REVERSE HAREM SERIES

ABOUT ABSORBING POISON

Return to the Veil and see what trouble holds next for Olivia and the descendants.

The age of dragons could be coming to an end—in five months to be exact. That is unless Olivia Campbell can collect all the kingdoms' stars to break the curse that has bound the remaining four dragon shifters to the Veil (a land unknown to humanity) for the last one hundred years.

After securing the Star of Tranquility, Olivia prepares for a journey deep into the woods of Viperus where Kieran Devenport reigns. Viperus thrives on tangled chaos and wild danger, and it will test Olivia's deepest fears to find the Star of Poison.

Kieran is edgy, charming, and deadly. His ability to breathe poison makes him a formidable foe or a powerful ally. Olivia is glad he is on her side, for her quest is not an easy one. The scorned witch, Tianna, is out for power . . . and blood.

But no matter the cost, Olivia is determined to save her dragons. Not even a sorceress filled with wrath can deter her. In fact, she can kiss her ass.

Four dragons.
One headstrong heroine.
And a reverse-harem fantasy romance that could change the fate of a dying race.

Absorbing Poison will transport fans of *Twilight*, *A Shade of Vampire*, and *The Curse of the Gods* to an enchanted world unlike any other.

Prepare for a unique spin on the lore you love and an adventure that is as thrilling as it is unexpected.

Scroll up and BUY NOW to begin . . .
*Recommended for ages 17+ due to language and sexual content.

DEDICATION

This book is for readers.
I wouldn't be able to do any of this without you!
I FLOVE you!

ACKNOWLEDGMENTS

First and foremost, I want to thank Stephany Wallace for being more than an incredible PA and editor, but also being my cheerleader and friend. I wouldn't get through my edits without those comments that make me lol.

Another huge thank you to Allisyn, who constantly helps me grow in my skills as a writer. I really do take all your notes to heart, even if it seems as if I'd forgotten them.

I want to give a big shoutout to the YA Vets. You know who you are. This group is a resource I can't do without. Muawah!

And as always, a massive thank you to the readers and reviewers. You guys give me the encouragement to keep doing this and making me believe in my dreams.
I FLOVE all of you!

1

Five. It is just a number. How could something so innocuous hold so much importance? It wasn't like we were talking about a gazillion. Many things can be associated with the number five.

It was the age I started kindergarten and demanded my mom braid my hair. It was the number of hotdogs Blake Cash ate in fifth grade on a dare, barfing all over the cafeteria. What had possessed me to sit at his table? It is the number of appendages most starfish have. It is how many senses humans are born with.

But most importantly, it was how many months I had left to break the dragon descendants' curse.

Jase, Kieran, Zade, and Issik—the four dragon shifters had swept me off the streets, bringing me to the Veil Isles, a place as dangerous as the breath of the descendants. Before I came along, there had been five descendants. Tianna, the witch who cursed the dragons, imprisoned the last of them on the isles for a hundred years, except for two days a year when they could cross the veil. She took Tobias's life—well, her curse did, to be more precise. He tested the boundaries of her spell, and paid the price with his life.

And now there were four.

My dragons.

Since we learned what Tianna wanted and how to break the curse, plans were put into motion. The question we needed to answer was: Whose kingdom did we venture to next, to find the stone that held each dragon's unique power? That discussion, of course, broke out into a brawl. Living with dragons had its downfalls. Shit got broken. A lot.

I had to intervene. What other choice did I have?

Throwing myself into the middle of a circle of dragons, I extended my arms into a *T*. "Wait, before you break another vase or start breathing fire. How about we solve this without violence?"

"Where is the fun in that?" Kieran asked in a sexy Irish accent, grinning like the fool he was.

Heaven forbid I suggest doing something practical. I glanced into Kieran's moss-green eyes. The color seemed brighter than usual, but I noticed that happened when he got fired up, which didn't happen often. The poison dragon was as lighthearted as they came. He was free-spirited, a joker, kind, and probably sang in the shower when no one was watching.

"Fine. Kill each other. Then I won't have to break this stupid curse."

"Stupid, huh?" Jase countered. He was opposite of Kieran in the circle, and I had to spin around to see him.

2

He shot me one of his famous raised dark brows. The dragon of Tranquility was smooth.

We were in Jase's study at Wakeland Keep. Zade had his arms folded over his broad chest, feet spread apart, and a scowl marring his full lips. Issik stood across from Zade like an immovable force. His blond hair was pulled back into some sort of man bun, keeping the silky locks off his gorgeous, but hard, face. It would take an act of God to cause Issik to flinch, or maybe flashing my boobs. That might work. He was frosty, not dead.

"Yes. When the four of you are acting like baboons, it's stupid." I scolded them, like a pack of two-year-olds.

None of them were fazed, least of all Zade. "Let me guess, you want us to pick stones again?" he asked.

"It worked well before," I defended with a shrug.

Four groans echoed through the room.

I rolled my eyes. "Fine, I have another suggestion. I'll close my eyes and Jase can spin me in a circle. When I open my eyes, whoever is directly in front of me gets to be the next victim."

I got no arguments. Amazeballs.

With that settled, I waited for Jase to put his hands on my shoulders. Zade, Kieran, and Issik shifted to even out the circle around me. It was like being burrito-wrapped in pure male sexiness. At Jase's touch, calmness radiated through me. After I closed my eyes, he spun me in multiple circles, and I lost my grip on gravity, my head spinning. His hands remained firmly on my shoulders to steady me. Otherwise, I would have stumbled like a drunken sailor.

When my eyes opened, I stared into irises as green as the rolling hills of Ireland.

Kieran—the dragon with the breath of poison.

"Hey, Blondie." Kieran's eyes traced over my face.

The warmth of Jase's body was still behind me, and the steady stream of serenity stemming from his hands still flowed over my shoulders. It seemed like second nature for him to use his gifts, especially when it came to me. "So, it's settled," Jase declared. "We go to Viperus next, to search for the Star of Poison."

That didn't sound ominous in the slightest. My enthusiasm was written all over my face.

Coming closer, Kieran lightly bumped his shoulder against mine, having to bend down to do so. "Don't worry. It's not as bad as it sounds."

"So there aren't creatures that could potentially eat, poison, or devour me?" I countered, being my usual smartass self.

Kieran's green hair was spiked down the center of his head, and the stud over his eye glittered under the waning sun streaming through the window. "No, there are, but you have four secret weapons: us."

That I did, and I would need all four of them to survive.

Releasing my shoulders, Jase walked to the desk. "We leave at first light. I know it doesn't need to be said, but we must be more alert than ever. Tianna is waiting for us to make a move. She'll do whatever it takes to get her hands on the stones."

The Star of Tranquility was carefully hidden away somewhere in Wakeland Keep. Not even I knew where it was, which was supposed to be for my own protection. At the mention of the witch, I shuddered. I was not looking forward to my next meeting with the redheaded whack job.

"Can't wait."

Did I say that out loud?

I did.

～

Wrapping the towel around my body, I secured it over my chest, tucking the terry cloth fabric in at the corners. I probably should have remembered to bring a change of clothes with me when I went to the bathing room, but such was my life. Forgetful should have been my first, middle, and last name. A closet full of pretty dresses sat in the corner of the room, but none of them were me. Give me sweats and a T-shirt, and I'd feel like a queen. I glared at the wardrobe door. Screw it. I was going to strut down the halls in nothing but a towel and pray for the best.

Still damp from the bath, I padded out into the hall. Coast was clear. Not a single descendant or staff member in sight. I exhaled and continued to the staircase. The halls of Wakeland Keep were drafty, scattering little goosebumps over my arms. It was very hopeful to think I would make it all the way to my room without being seen. The descendants were preparing to make the journey to Viperus—Kieran's kingdom. Hot Lips was my next dragon-curse-breaking victim. I might have been able to accidentally stumble upon the Star of Tranquility, but it was outlandish of them to think I could do it a second time. Or a third. Or a fourth!

They were all freaking nuts.

I was nearly as clueless as the first day I arrived in the Veil Isles. The only difference was I knew dragons were real, witches sucked, and I was probably never going home again. Finding the Star had been sheer dumb luck. I didn't have some kind of magical compass that pointed me in the right direction. I wanted more than anything to free the descendants from Tianna's curse. To give them back the life that had been stolen from them. To allow them to live, instead of constantly searching for ways to release themselves from the chains that kept them locked to the isles…

But how the hell was *I* going to find the next Star?

The four of them looked at me with hope and expectancy. I liked it better without the pressure. Now, I couldn't fail them.

I'd become so lost in my own head that I hadn't been paying attention to where I was going. Stopping dead in my tracks, I glanced around the long, dimly lit corridor, trying to determine where I'd wandered off to now. This didn't look like my hallway. In fact, I wasn't sure I'd ever been to this part of Jase's castle.

Fabulous. My last few hours in Wakeland Keep and I got lost. I swore to God, I didn't purposely do this shit.

Nibbling on my lower lip, I turned left and then right, deciding which way I should venture. Did it matter? I should sit down and stay put until one of the dragons found me. I'd have better luck of that happening, than finding my own way back.

A sigh escaped my mouth as I tightened my hold on the white towel, offering me little warmth. Did I really want to wait for one of them? If I did, I would have to listen to how I still couldn't find my way around, and that I needed a babysitter at all times. Blah. Blah. Blah.

I could actually hear their voices in my head.

Olivia, what are you doing?

Wow, that was way too real. It had sounded like Kieran was directly behind me.

Determining my best bet was to go back the way I came, I spun around, and ran into a wall of muscle. Kieran's husky laugh washed over me. The next thing I knew, my arms were flailing in the air, tangling with the descendant's as he scrambled to catch me. Not the smartest move. His reaction was a tad too slow, on account of him laughing at me. Legs got mixed in there as well, and then we were falling.

We went down in a heap. Somehow, Kieran managed to protect me from breaking my neck. I don't know how he contorted his body with such speed and accuracy, but he cushioned the brunt of my impact with his body. He was still chuckling, when I blew the damp tendrils of hair out of my eyes to stare down at his face.

He smelled delicious, like a woodsy waterfall, earthy and sweet. I basked in his scent, letting it encompass me wholly. I wanted to press my lips into the curve of his neck. Maybe I could ask him to carry me to my room. I wouldn't get lost, and I would get the added benefit of staying in his arms longer. Before offering the suggestion, I noticed he was distracted. His eyes weren't focused on me, but elsewhere.

The towel secured around me had slipped free, baring my breasts to the world, or in this case, Kieran's face. If he so much as moved a fraction to the left or right, he could have done wicked things that would have my body engulfed in flames, and not the kind Zade breathed.

I was stunned, but for a moment. A squeal flew from my mouth as I attempted to fix the towel and cover myself, but I made matters worse. My knee bumped into something, and I was afraid of what it might be.

His arms came around me, halting my squirming. I narrowed my eyes at him. He wore his shit-eating grin. "Stop moving, Blondie. You're making this more enticing for me."

I gasped as my fears were confirmed. "That isn't a cell phone in your front pocket?"

A chuckle rumbled his chest, vibrating my still bare boobs. "Definitely not, and if you don't want to find out more about it, I suggest you figure out a way to remove yourself from atop of me, without exposing more of yourself. Not that I mind the view." His green eyes blazed, brightening the longer I stared at him.

For the love of dragon's breath. Why do things like this keep happening to me?

My entire body sank into his, and I stayed motionless while I contemplated my options to remove myself and still keep my dignity, if that was even possible. Why couldn't he be flabby and have a potbelly like some guys get from drinking too much beer? Nope. Kieran had to be ripped and firm in all the right places.

The worst part: I was still mostly naked. "You can stop

grinning," I grumbled at him. He was finding the entire situation far too amusing for my liking.

"You have beautiful breasts. They're perfect. You shouldn't hide them."

"I bet you would love that."

The grin on his lips spread. "I don't know a guy who wouldn't."

I couldn't believe we were spread out in the hall, discussing my boobs. Had there ever been a more awkward conversation in the history of dragon-kind?

Before I could say another thing, a dark shadow appeared over me. "What are the two of you doing on the floor? And why is Olivia naked? Or do I want to know?" Jase scowled, hovering over us, his voice deep and formidable.

Rushing to my feet, I jumped off Kieran to stand. My fingers scrambled to keep the towel from falling to the ground, but at this point, modesty had been thrown out the window. Why did I even bother?

I brought the white fabric up around the popular topic of the hour. I'd be happy to never talk about my boobs again. Ever.

"Nothing is going on. I fell," I quickly explain, my cheeks stained pink.

"On top of Kieran… naked?" Jase asked.

Kieran laughed and pushed himself to his feet, doing nothing to aid the situation. It seemed like he wanted Jase to think something was going on between us. This whole thing with the descendants was difficult to navigate. I didn't understand my feelings or how to deal with the four of them.

"Yes," I ground out, a damp strand of hair falling over my shoulder.

Kieran shoved his hands in his pockets, rocking back on his heels. "She's telling the truth. I found her wandering the halls, and the next thing I knew, she was on top of me with her chest in my face."

A shiver ran down my spine, but not from the cold this time. "Can we stop talking about my boobs for five seconds?"

"No," they both responded.

I'd had enough. "The discussion of my boobs is officially off-limits. Got it? This doesn't need to become one of those funny stories you tease me about later."

Kieran and Jase grinned at me. This was definitely one of those stories they were never going to let me forget. I groaned. Things had gone from sensual to awkward, to dire in mere seconds.

"I should get ready to leave."

"Do you need help getting dressed?" Kieran winked.

"If I didn't need this towel, I would whack you with it." I clutched the soft material as I collected my composure and stormed down the corridor. I still wasn't sure if I was heading in the right direction, but it didn't matter as long as no one was staring at my chest.

It took me ten more minutes to find my room, but the important thing was I had, and was safely tucked away behind closed doors—no dragons to make me feel like my emotions were tied to the end of a yo-yo. I didn't bother to put clothes on, but face-planted onto the bed as I let out a muffled shriek of mild annoyance and extreme embarrassment.

There. I'd had my momentary freak-out of the day. I had more pressing matters to attend to now. I'd been warned that the journey into Viperus's woods would be dangerous, not only because Tianna would use every opportunity to acquire what she desired, but the kingdom itself was perilous. Like the waters of Wakeland, the woods of Viperus were home to some unsavory creatures. The mention of snakes gave me the willies.

I shuddered thinking about it.

Letting out a pent up breath, I rolled off the bed to gather what little possessions I wanted to take with me. I slipped into the clothes I had arrived in—jeans, a T-shirt, and boots. If I would be traipsing around in the woods, I put my foot down on wearing a dress fit for a goddess. And to be honest, wearing my clothes gave me a sense of security, making me feel like myself, not like someone who was chosen to break a curse. Even though the material was washed, I could still smell me on it. Nostalgia and sadness whipped through me. Not a day went by that I didn't think about my mom, but in moments like these, when I was feeling alone and scared, it hit me harder.

Stiffening my chin, I refocused my mind on the menial tasks of tidying the room, and stuffing the few things I had into my bag. In a few hours, we'd be leaving for Viperus and the pressure was on.

No big deal.

I got this.

But I didn't believe a single word of it. Inside, I was trembling.

I took one last sweeping glance around my room. What had once been a prison was now a sanctuary. Leaving Wakeland was harder than I'd anticipated. I'd assumed I wouldn't form any real attachment to the kingdom I'd lived in for the last month, but I was wrong. After living on my own, not answering to anyone and homeless, I realized how much I'd been craving a family. And whether I had been looking for them or not, a family—no matter how unorthodox—was exactly what the descendants had given me.

It isn't the place that makes you feel safe. It's Jase, Kieran, Zade, and Issik, I reminded myself. If we were together, I'd be okay.

Taking a deep breath, I snatched my bag off the bed and swung it over my shoulder. I walked across the room and stepped over the threshold, heading to what was probably going to be my doom. Not the kind of positive attitude I should have, but some days it was hard to keep your chin up, when the task in front of you seemed so far from reach and daunting.

Downstairs, the four dragons waited in the great hall. Zade paced across the floor, muttering to himself, probably grumbling about how long it was taking me. Issik leaned against the wall, looking bored. Kieran stared out the window, and Jase was in the corner, lounging in a leather chair. I could tell tensions were high, and they were anxious to get going. No one wanted to find the next stone more than the four of them. Their lives depended on it.

"Who's ready for a little adventure?" I asked with a fake smile, as I sauntered into the center of the room.

Jase's violet eyes swept over me, brimming with exasperation. "This isn't a vacation or a camping trip."

"Good thing. I've never done either," I replied, looping my backpack over both my shoulders.

Four sets of eyes stared at me.

Shifting the straps on my back higher, I shrugged. "I'm not a fan of nature or flying, at least I wasn't before."

Kieran's pierced lips curled. "Imagine that. Olivia afraid of flying. You seem to have overcome that fear fairly quickly."

Yeah well, I kind of didn't have a choice, living with four dragons. "Watch it, or I'll hit you with my tranquility breath."

Kieran shook his head, but the smile on his lips didn't dull. "We need to teach you how to control your gift, without putting all the isles to sleep."

"And how are you going to do that?" It had been a few days since I found the Star of Tranquility and absorbed its power, giving me the same ability as Jase—to put people in a deep slumber. But I had no idea how it worked, or how to control this sleeping spell bestowed upon me.

As Kieran and I talked about my newfound ability to breathe tranquility, Jase, Issik, and Zade surrounded me, herding me out into the hall while Kieran kept me engaged in the conversation. It wasn't until the breeze rolling off the sea washed over my face, that I noticed we were outside the castle.

My feet stopped moving, staring at the vast trees towering in front of us. "We're really doing this?"

"We are, Little Warrior." Issik's cool voice tickled my right ear, and then we were moving again, straight toward the dense forest.

I cast a glance over my shoulder, toward the castle for memory's sake. Harlow stood in the doorway, eyeing me with disdain, and if I wasn't mistaken, her eyes glistened with tears. It could have been a trick played by the sun, but I didn't think so. She had a thing for Jase. Because of her treatment of me last month, it was hard for me to feel sympathetic. I definitely wasn't going to miss her sunny disposition. One good thing about going to Viperus was, I didn't have to worry about Harlow trying to stab me in my sleep.

The woods of Viperus bordered the southern part of Wakeland. Not long after we entered the towering trees, the air no longer smelled of sea and moisture, but of pine and earth. I'd made this trek once before when the descendants had taken me to the temple of their fathers. The journey was still burned in my memory.

"Why aren't we flying again?" I asked, tripping over a

stupid twig for the twentieth time. The woods held us in a tight embrace, making me feel claustrophobic. I wanted space and air.

Zade strode up beside me, dwarfing me with his six-foot-plus frame, a scowl twisting his lips. "Tianna will expect us to be moving. She might not know which kingdom we've chosen, but you can bet your cute little butt she will have scouts watching."

"Can we leave Olivia's butt out of it?" Kieran called over his shoulder, amusement sparkling in his voice. He was leading the group, striding a few paces in front of us, and eager to get home. Who could blame him?

I ignored the comment about my butt. Too much talk about my body parts had already occurred, and I wasn't going to add fuel to the fire, but the tug at the corner of Jase's lips had me on edge. If I didn't steer the conversation back on topic, it would derail to my ass or, worse yet, my boobs. Hell no. I'd had enough embarrassment today. "But doesn't she want me to find the stones?"

"Yes and no," Jase added, clearing up absolutely nothing.

It was probably a waste of time trying to get inside the head of an evil sorceress, but what else did I have to do while schlepping through the woods? A couple of thoughts popped into my head, but none of them were suitable for hiking in the forest, and ironically, they all involved me nearly naked.

What is going on with me? I've suddenly become sex crazed.

Since the other night with the towel mishap, it seemed like all I could think about was getting naked. I couldn't stop reliving that moment… with a different ending. One where I didn't run away. One where Jase stayed. And the three of us...

Dear God, how much longer was this trip?

My cheeks deepened in color, and I prayed no one would notice. "That doesn't make any sense," I said to Jase, trying to reel in my thoughts.

"We're dealing with a witch. It's not supposed to make sense," Zade pointed out then.

And dealing with four dragons is?

"Are you feeling okay? You're looking a little flushed." Issik, the guy of few words, watched me with his piercing blue eyes. His blond hair was swept into a ponytail, making him look like a Viking warrior.

Damn these dragons and their ability to feel my emotions. It wasn't fair. Here I was tasked with freeing them from their cursed prison, and they got rewarded by having a direct gateway to my feelings. Since they had tasted my blood, a bond had formed between them and me. It was one-sided and unfair as hell. Each shifter could sense a different one of my emotions. Jase got fear, Zade anger, Issik sadness, and Kieran passion. But there seemed to be a bit of wiggle room.

"I'm fine," I grumbled, dragging my feet through a pile of fallen leaves.

"Here, drink this." Jase held out a container of water.

I took a swig and handed it back to Jase. Water was precious but also heavy, and I'd chosen not to bring any with me. It was hard enough carrying my own possessions and staying upright. "So what's it like in Viperus?" I directed my question to Kieran, suddenly feeling the need to be a Chatty Cathy.

"Buggy." It was Zade who responded.

"Green." Issik added, then.

Jase couldn't be left out, of course. "Untamed."

They all had their opinions of Kieran's kingdom, and I found it interesting that none of them sounded thrilled with the destination. Whereas my hesitation had little to do with the kingdom itself, the other three seemed leery of it, but then again, Kieran *was* a poison dragon.

"Don't listen to them. Viperus is lush and vibrant—full of life." Kieran defended his home with so much pride, that his chest swelled with it as he walked. "The plants that thrive in this part of the isles provide us with air to breathe, and rich soil for the cultivation of food."

"Do you have any crazy jealous girlfriends waiting to carve out my eyeballs?" I inquired. It was a justified question after my stay at Wakeland Keep.

"We give all the crazy girls to Jase." Kieran winked at me.

"Wonderful," Jase muttered, but his eyes twinkled with good humor.

I chuckled, some of the tension leaving my body, but the small reprieve of stress didn't last long.

Squawk. Squawk.

Dark shadows above the trees swooped down, their wings skimming the tops of the branches and shaking the leaves. All four descendants stopped and formed an immediate circle around me, causing the air in my lungs to stall.

Is it Tianna?

Has she found us?

The boys surrounding me tensed; ready to shift at any

17

second if the need presented itself. An uneasy silence fell between us. My heart hammered in my chest as I waited to see what the creatures would do next. Time dragged by, and I was positive whatever was flying above our heads would swoop down and whisk me off my feet at any moment.

"It was a pair of day bats," Jase announced, his wide shoulders relaxing.

The others were quick to follow, stepping out of their defensive positions. "We might have gotten lucky this time, but you can bet Tianna is out there. We need to keep moving." Issik's raspy, cold voice had me forgetting my smaller problems.

No matter how much my feet and thighs protested, I pushed on without complaining. Walking had been something I'd done daily when I was homeless, but tromping through the woods of Viperus was strenuous. It could have been due to the numerous times I tripped. Each time I stumbled over a twig, a rock, or my own two feet, I swore one of the dragons would throw me over their shoulders any minute. We would have covered more ground faster if they had.

For the next few hours, things were quiet, and it gave me the chance to think. A scary place. Things should have felt easier now that we knew what we were looking for, but not in the fucking jungle. Viperus was vast and wild, and staring at the never-ending forest made it seem hopeless. How the hell was I supposed to find a tiny stone in here? Where was I supposed to begin? We hadn't even reached the castle yet and I wanted to give up so badly.

But then the descendants turned to fence me in from all sides, watching me with curious expressions.

Jase leaned in close. "Do I dare ask what you're thinking about?"

"I was thinking how impossible it's going to be for me to locate a single crystal in all this." My hands swept out over the woodlands. What was the point of trying to deny or hide what I felt? They could sense something was upsetting me anyway.

"We don't expect you to do this alone, Cupcake," Jase reassured me. "Don't despair. Let's take this one day at a time. Deal?"

"And as dragons, we can cover a lot of ground," Zade reminded me from behind me.

That was true, and it did make me feel slightly better, until I noticed Jase touching me. His hand had slipped behind my neck. "Jase," I rumbled.

Jase removed his hand, but not before giving me a little extra boost of relaxation. "You looked like you needed a pick-me-up."

Who could fault him for that? My mind had been traveling to a dark place. "We really are in the middle of nowhere," I remarked, admiring and feeling intimidated by the endless sprawl of woods surrounding us.

"Don't worry," Kieran assured me. "It's not as scary as they make it sound."

Kieran may not have believed his kingdom was eerie, but it would take more than his reassurance to shake the uneasiness that had settled over me. Deep down, we were all unsure about the next stage of the curse, and how it would affect our lives. The thought made me uncertain of the path we'd set ourselves on, or maybe it was that I couldn't shake the hunch we were being watched. By Tianna no doubt. The witch had spies everywhere, and she was biding her time, waiting for the right moment to strike.

I swiveled to look behind me while walking backward. I didn't know what possessed me to do such a thing, but Tianna had me on edge. On my next step, the ground was suddenly gone.

"Olivia!" Issik bellowed. He had been standing on my left, and his hands flew out to make a grab for me, but it was too late.

I was falling, and the scream that ripped from my throat echoed the entire way down.

Oomph.

I hit the ground, landing awkwardly on top of my foot, which was followed by a shooting pain, powerful enough to have me crying out loud. For a few terrifying seconds, I didn't move a muscle.

"Olivia!" boomed four voices from above my head.

A surge of anxiety tumbled through me. *I think I'm alive. I think I survived. Ninety percent sure I'm not dead.*

These were the thoughts that ran through my head as I took stock of what happened, and how I ended up underground. I'd twisted the hell out of my ankle; the rest of my injuries were scrapes and bruises—nothing that wouldn't heal—but damn if it didn't hurt like fatal wounds.

Cradling my ankle with one hand, I lifted my other hand to my temple and winced. My hand jerked away, blood staining my fingers. *Fucking fabulous.*

"I'm alive," I yelled up, hoping they would hear me. I deliberately left out the details of my injuries, knowing they would do something irrational to save me. But what I really wanted to say was, *Come get me before I bleed to death.* That wasn't an actual concern, except for in my head.

"Stay where you are. We're coming down to get you," Jase ordered me in his stern voice.

I had assumed they would, but it gave me comfort to hear them say it. Trying to breathe through the panic, I pushed slowly to my feet and grimaced, clenching my teeth as I put weight on my right foot.

"Shit," I hissed, my hand reaching out to steady myself on the rocky wall. My ankle was definitely injured.

My eyes swept the dark space, surveying my unexpected surroundings. I wanted to ensure I wasn't in any immediate danger. And with that thought, my mind drummed up a slew of horrendous situations, the hole caving in, being mauled to death by an ogre, twisting my other ankle trying to escape.

As I stepped out of the little grassy area I had landed on, I emerged into a cavern like nothing I could have ever imagined. Rock walls arched to high above my head from all sides, but they weren't ordinary stones. Flecks of green crystals shone like a million stars, twinkling underground. My mouth dropped open as my eyes scanned the open cave.

Holy dragon's breath! What is this place?

I felt like I'd struck gold.

Sounds of flowing water ricocheted off the stone, luring me farther into the cavern. Around the corner, a stream of water ran through a dark tunnel. The water emitted a green glow and lit up the pathway. I hobbled up to its edge and sat down, relieved to give my throbbing ankle a break. This was as good a spot as any to wait for the descendants. From behind me, I could hear pebbles and dirt moving about. It would be a matter of minutes before the descendants rescued me.

As I stared into the mesmerizing waters, a familiar hum trembled over the surface. Deep within the water was the sound of a woman singing in a hypnotic voice. The volume of her song was like a quiet whisper, and I strained to catch the words. Blinking, I determined I wasn't going crazy when a woman's face materialized in the pattern of the waves.

Long blonde hair haloed around her oval-shaped face as she came into focus. She looked like a mermaid floating under the water's surface, her skin glittering, but she had feet. They stuck out from under her flowing white dress.

"Olivia," she sang my name, a soft smile on her lips. She had an unusual lilt to her voice, like an ancient tongue no longer spoken. "You must save him," she begged me. Urgency was reflected in her green eyes.

"How?" I replied, my fingers gripping the rocky edge of the riverbank. I didn't know which descendant she was speaking about, but it didn't matter as long as I got a step closer to finding the Star of Poison, and if this woman had any information to help me, she better start spilling her spooky guts.

Her smile turned sad. "The stone you seek is buried deep in the unseen, but in plain sight for anyone to see."

How was I supposed to make any sense out of that babble? "I don't understand. Can't you just tell me where to look?"

Her face was bathed in a green glow from the water.

"But I have. It's you, and only you, who have the power to do what must be done. The Stars have chosen you."

What did that say about the Stars? I didn't know how much stock I could put in them, if they picked me. I was no hero. "Who are you?" I whispered, extending my hand into the water. I wanted to know if she was real, a mirage, or a ghost. In the isles, you could never be sure.

The woman sank farther down, away from my touch and into the depths of the dark waters. I could no longer see her, but her voice rose up to me. "We'll guide you when we can. Take comfort in that."

Who were these women I kept seeing in the water? This one was different than the one in Wakeland, yet there was a similarity about the two of them. I believed they wanted to help me, regardless of their uncanny methods.

"Olivia?" a deep voice called, breaking through the bewitching encounter.

"Issik?" I croaked. He crouched down in front of me, staring at me with ice blue eyes of worry. I threw myself into his arms, never more ready to get out of this cave. His coolness encompassed me as his strong arms came around me. "What took you so long?" I murmured against his neck.

"Did you hit your head?" His fingers gently framed either side of my face, and he examined the cut above my brow. The frown marring his lips darkened.

Instinctively, I leaned one cheek into his touch. "I'm okay, but I twisted my ankle."

Slipping his hands under my legs, he lifted me, securing me against his chest. My arms automatically looped around the base of his neck. "Let's get you out of here before you do any more damage to yourself."

A chill entered his voice, making me wonder what I had done other than fall into a cave. Was he annoyed at the delay in our journey? Was he worried about me? Or was he just being Issik—cold and aloof? Even so, I knew Issik cared for me... Well, I thought he did most of the time. Of the descendants, Issik remained the hardest for me to understand.

The side of my face rested against his, wanting to thaw the chill that radiated from the ice prince. "I'm sorry," I apologized. For what, I didn't know, but it seemed like the appropriate response.

He tilted his head slightly, aligning our lips. My pulse quickened, and all I could think was, *Issik is going to kiss me.* Our breaths mingled, and our lips hovered there for a few heart-stopping seconds. The cave disappeared; the pain in my ankle vanished; and my mind filled with nothing but thoughts of Issik's lips on mine. The yearning to know how he tasted consumed me.

I should have known better. The ice prince had a resolve of steel. He was the only descendant who hadn't kissed me, and I couldn't help but wonder if he didn't desire me the same way I did him. I gave up pretending I didn't want to spend every waking moment locking lips with one of them. Who wouldn't? They were far too attractive for their own good.

The luster in his ice blue eyes faded as he turned his face forward again and continued walking. "You have nothing to be sorry for. It's Kieran who should be apologizing." His tone was gruff.

I tried to hide my disappointment, but it leaked into my voice anyway. "Why is that?"

"This is his domain. If he spent less time flirting with you, he would have sensed the change in the landscape. He should have been able to warn you."

Issik blamed Kieran. Of their own accord, my fingers twirled the loose strands of hair at the nape of his neck. I was compelled to touch him, and Issik didn't seem to mind.

"It was an accident."

He scowled. "You seem to have more accidents than normal humans."

I shrugged, a smile tugging at my lips. "Probably, but if I hadn't fallen, then you wouldn't be carrying me, and I kind of like being in your arms."

Issik's eyes flew to mine, and my heart pounded all over the place. When he looked at me like that, being stuck in a cave didn't seem so bad. "You're something else."

"So I've been told." Since kissing was off the menu, I inquired about something he said. "What do you mean Kieran would have been able to sense the hole?"

With ease, he moved us through the cavern toward the grassy patch. "We have a connection to our kingdoms through our dragon blood. The land is as much a part of us as the scales covering our bodies, or the breath we expel."

Fascinating. The more I learned about the descendants, the more I was convinced they couldn't be real—that I would wake up one day back on the streets, and everything that happened to me would be nothing but a dream.

"What kind of stone is this?" I asked, dazzled by the flecks of emerald we walked past.

"Did you touch it?" Issik asked with a sudden sharpness to his tone that took me aback.

I shook my head. "No."

His brows furrowed. "As pretty as the crystals look, they are poisonous."

I should have known. Kieran had warned me that Viperus was filled with plants, animals, and elements that could be lethal to humans.

We came to the spot where I'd fallen. "You ready to get out of here?"

Squinting against the beams of sunlight, I glanced upward. My other dragons waited for me above, and the sight made my chest swell. What would I do without them? "I thought you'd never ask."

The descendants made a makeshift ladder out of themselves, positioned every six to seven feet along the rocky wall. In their dragon form, they never would have fit through the hole. Issik lifted me up, handing me off to Jase. "Careful, she's injured her ankle," the Ice Prince told Dimples.

"What are we going to do with you, Cupcake?" he muttered, holding me in his grasp. He gave me a long squeeze before passing me to Zade.

Heat encased me. "We'll get your ankle fixed up, Little Gem."

Last was Kieran. Safeguarded in his arms, he easily lifted us out, but he didn't immediately let me go. Instead, he tugged me into his lap while he hugged me to death. "You scared the crap out of me, Blondie." His voice was like a whispered caress over my body.

I shivered, but not from the near brush with death. The descendants had a way of talking to me that made me feel seduced each time one of them opened their mouth. It could have been the stupidest of phrases and I would swoon. *It's raining today. What's for dinner? Olivia, are you listening to me?* I was a puddle of goo in their presence.

A light breeze ruffled my hair. "I scared the crap out of myself."

The others had made it out, hovering over Kieran and me. "We told you it was dangerous," Jase scolded me.

My neck craned to look up at the other three. "I thought you meant bears, snakes, and tigers, oh my, not that I would fall to the center of the earth."

Kieran's and Zade's chests rumbled. Jase's eyes twinkled with humor, but Issik's lips kept their straight line. "You didn't fall through the world," Jase assured me. "It is a chasm."

"Oh, in that case," I snapped back. Wiggling off Kieran, I pushed to my feet and instantly regretted it. Pain spiked through my ankle—a jolting reminder of why I needed to stay off my feet.

"We'll take turns carrying you," Jase announced, swooping in to cradle me against his chest, without me having to say anything. I had four of the most attentive boyfriends in the world.

"Why do you get to go first?" Zade complained, his possessiveness roaring to life.

They were arguing over me, a pattern I should be

getting used to, competition ran fiercely among them. They had once been rival princes, though their current circumstance had thrown them together, forging a deep friendship.

As soon as Jase grabbed me, I knew I didn't want to be hauled around the woods like a swaddled infant. "Put me down. I can walk."

Jase already strode through the woods, expecting the others to follow. "Not going to happen, Cupcake."

I pouted at him, but he was staring at me with a dark and gloomy expression in return. "Why are you looking at me like that?"

"You're bleeding," he replied, the violet in his eyes becoming intense.

I touched my temple, remembering the cut. "It's just a scratch. I'm fine." The throbbing would eventually go away... I hoped. To distract myself from the pain, I pressed my hand over his heart, wanting to comfort him.

At the mention of my blood, Zade was suddenly at our side, cinnamon eyes searching my face. "We don't like it when you're hurt," he stated.

That made two of us... or actually, five. The dragons all wore identical frowns.

Issik, eager to get moving, pushed through the thick undergrowth of Viperus. The rest of the descendants shook their heads but followed.

I was passed from Jase to Zade to Kieran over the next few hours. One moment we were picking our way through overgrown thorns and brush, and then suddenly the path opened up again. Kieran set me down, allowing me to get my first real glimpse of the castle. My footsteps faltered, and I gasped. Up close, the castle was both impressive and frightening. The once white stone had become mottled with dark green, weathered from the infiltration of vines and moss. Torches lit up the walls, the soft glow of it a welcoming sight.

My eyes scanned left and right, trying to take everything in at once. "Holy crap," I muttered.

"It's something else, isn't?" Kieran replied, his voice coming from right behind me.

Words failed me. It wasn't only the sheer size of Viperus Keep that left me stranded in Stunned City. It was also the enormous stone statue of a viper that wound its way around the castle from the base to the tip-top of the highest tower.

Before I had a chance to mentally prepare myself for living inside a keep with a snake as the mascot, Kieran grabbed me by the waist, drawing me into the open field toward his home. "You're going to love it here, Blondie."

I highly doubted it, still, I didn't have the heart to tell him how uncertain I felt, but Jase knew. The tranquility dragon came up on the other side of me, taking my free hand in his. An instantaneous stream of calm flowed through my blood. Jase gave me a small smile of encouragement, using his gift to make me relax.

"Welcome to Viperus, Blondie," Kieran announced. Moonlight shone on the side of his face.

Zade's amber eyes flickered down to me. "If anything tries to bite me in my sleep, I'm setting it on fire," he mumbled.

Of course I could count on Zade to plant such a welcoming thought in my head.

"Don't be such a baby," Issik retorted, a small smile cracking his blank mask, before he strutted into the grassy clearing.

With Jase and Kieran's help, I hobbled through the front door of the castle. My pride was happy to be walking. As for first impressions, I didn't want to be seen as someone who couldn't stand on her own two feet. I wanted the staff at Viperus to respect me. The last thing I needed was another Harlow making things difficult. I didn't want any drama or trouble. Enough of that reigned in my life with the curse.

An elderly robust woman waited excitedly for Kieran's return. She reminded me of my grandma when she'd been alive. Her soft gray hair was fixed in a messy bun. Her brown eyes glowed at the sight of Kieran as she held her arms open wide.

A childish grin split his face. "Alice." Kieran picked her up, spinning her in a circle.

"Put me down, you imp." She playfully whacked him with a dish towel. From the smear of flour above her brow, she had just come from the kitchen. Kieran set her back down on her feet. "We've been preparing your favorite dinner, knowing how hungry the five of you would be after the day of travel." She in turn, gave each of the other dragons a long hug, before her sparkling brown eyes landed on me. "You must be Olivia."

I nodded, holding out my hand. "It's nice to meet you."

"She has manners, will you look at that. Not like the others you bring around here." I found myself engulfed in a warm hug. She smelled of cookies, sweet and homey.

I pinned Kieran with a look. *Others*, I mouthed.

Kieran cleared his throat. "Not to worry. They weren't who we were searching for."

Alice kept an arm around my shoulder and gave it a squeeze. "Ah, yes. But she is, I hear. And she's as lovely as a peach."

I adored Alice already.

The inside of Viperus Keep was laid out similarly to Jase's castle, which I found a blessing, but that was where the similarities ended. All of the doorway arches came to a point with the windows mirroring their tapered design, reminding me of a cathedral. Large chandeliers hung from the vaulted ceilings in the great room, casting soft flickers of light over the earth-toned tiled floors, and vines crept from the outside in, encasing the columns in green foliage and trimming the ceilings like garland.

"I can't believe you live here," I told Kieran, spinning around the room in awe.

"It's pretty spectacular. As a kid, I spent hours exploring the woods," he confessed, looking at the other dragons like they were wimps for being wary.

It was hard to think of them as little boys, given how long they'd lived, but I imagined the four of them were quite the troublemakers for their parents. And now they had lived on the isles for almost a hundred years, their lives frozen by a curse.

"I hope you brought your appetite, dear," Alice offered, looping an arm around my shoulders. She guided me farther into the castle, while the descendants followed close behind.

"I'm starved," I admitted.

Alice clucked her tongue. "Didn't they feed you in Wakeland?"

Jase made a snorting sound in the back of his throat.

How much did Alice know about me? She seemed to be well informed. Just how did Kieran have the time to come here and fill Alice in on all the details of my life? It was obvious Alice was someone he trusted.

We followed her into the kitchen where we were met by the fragrant smells of a feast. A girl with curly mahogany hair labored at the stove, peeling apples. A variety of pans steamed with meats, greens and potatoes rested atop the stove.

"Take a seat, and be quick about it before the food gets cold," Alice instructed us. "I won't let any of you go to bed hungry."

"You never do, Alice," Zade answered, taking a seat at the wooden table in the center of the room.

Chairs scraped as the rest of us sat. It seemed no matter where I was, the four of them surrounded me, but in a good way. I'd come to depend on it... on them. Two of the girls working in the kitchen appeared around us, each holding a plate of food. In a matter of minutes, the table was filled with meats, potatoes, fruits, breads, and other vegetables. It all looked delicious, and I wasn't sure where to start. I piled my plate, knowing my eyes were bigger than my belly.

As we ate, the four dragons caught Alice up on our last encounter with Tianna. No matter my efforts to dispel her from my mind, she wormed her way into my thoughts. Issik mistook my tiredness for fear… or so I told myself.

He leaned in close. "Don't worry about Tianna. We'll make sure she doesn't get to you."

And how did they propose to do that? She was a witch with magical means at her fingertips. I trusted the descendants without question, but there were some places not even they could shield me from Tianna—my dreams being one of those undefendable spots. Since the night she came for the Star of Tranquility, I hadn't been able to sleep. It wasn't a matter of if, but when, she'd pop back into our lives.

I pushed the potatoes around on my plate. "I know," I retorted, forcing myself to give Issik a small smile.

"How long do you think before she comes back for the stone?" Kieran asked the others. "We know she isn't about to give up that easily."

"No, that isn't Tianna's style. We'll worry about that when the time comes. For now, let's keep our focus on finding the Star of Poison," Jase instructed, his violet eyes catching mine briefly.

I swallowed. For the remainder of the meal, I stayed silent, listening to the four dragons strategize. It was obvious they had done this often, sitting around the dinner table discussing how they were going to kill Tianna. For me, plotting someone's death was a discomforting topic, even if the bitch deserved it.

Alice and the other two girls cleared the table, refusing

to let me lift a finger, but having people wait on me made me uncomfortable. I didn't like not being able to pull my weight.

Issik stood at the same time I did, putting a hand at the small of my back when my legs wobbled. My ankle still throbbed, and my feet were blistered. "You look tired, Little Warrior," he stated, lines of worry creasing his forehead.

"You have no idea," I replied, leaning against his shoulder for support.

His hand slipped to my waist, partly lifting me up so my feet barely touched the ground, taking the pressure off my ankle. "To bed you go."

As glorious as a bed sounded, I longed for a bath to rid myself of the dirt, blood, and grime. "Any chance I could bathe before you tuck me in?" I asked wryly, as we left the kitchen with the others directly behind us.

"We could all use a shower," Kieran agreed with a wicked smile.

"That wasn't quite what I had in mind," I mumbled, shooting down the roguish dragon's insinuation.

"God, a shower would do wonders," Zade added, a look of longing sliding into his handsome features.

"You're telling me," Issik grunted, wrinkling his nose. "I can smell you from here. It's not pretty."

Zade cocked a dark brow, mischief in his gaze. "Is that so?"

I shook my head at the two shifters. "Fine, we'll all shower, just don't give each other bloody lips before we get there."

Four dragon mouths dropped open. "Is she serious?"

Jase muttered, a look of surprise springing into his expression.

Kieran grinned. "Don't question it."

I rolled my eyes. Issik and I trailed behind the rest of them as we meandered through the castle. Kieran's home was like living in a greenhouse. The sound of gushing water tickled my ears as we reached a set of oversized double doors. Carved into the wood were a pair of ornate snakes twining into the shape of a *V*. Kieran pushed open the doors, revealing a beautiful, gently flowing waterfall. It rained over a cliff, dropping into a basin of fresh water, enclosed by swooping vines and bordered with white and blue wildflowers. The air smelled of clean moisture and sweet honeysuckle. Steam billowed from the basin.

My mouth dropped open in pure wonderment. "This is the shower?"

"Not too shabby," Zade whispered in my ear, his hot breath trailing down my neck.

Issik helped me approach the bank, and I held out my fingers, letting the stream of water run over my hand. The temperature was perfect.

"I want to live here. Right in this room."

Kieran chuckled. "It's yours to use whenever you like."

"I'm going to be the cleanest person in Viperus," I replied, grinning. Unlike the first time Kieran brought me to the bathhouse in Wakeland, I didn't hesitate to shed my clothes. It wasn't as if they hadn't seen me naked before, and I was absolutely dying to lose the sweat and grime. Flipping off my shoes and socks, I touched my bare feet to the rocky ground, which was smoother than it appeared.

My shirt and pants were quick to follow, and I left them where they fell, leaving me in my undergarments.

Kieran folded his arms, not bothering to turn around while I made my way to the water, but neither did the others. Wading in, I closed my eyes and sighed in delight. I was bathing in utopia. Moving into the waterfall, the water cascaded over my face. This might have been worth the day of hell in the jungle.

When I opened my eyes, the four of them stood on the edge of the basin, watching me with mixed expressions. "What are you waiting for?" I called out to them, smoothing my wet hair off my face.

Suddenly, they were scrambling to disrobe and get into the water, like it was a race for the last slice of pizza in the world. I giggled, but the sound was overpowered by the splashes of the descendants jumping into the basin. Like a tidal wave, a surge of water came rushing right for me, and my laughter was washed away as I was pulled under. I came through the surface to find Kieran beside me.

"You look like a mermaid." His husky voice sent goosebumps over my arms. He came through the waterfall, dipping his head under the spray of water. His thick lashes stuck together, emphasizing the hue of his green eyes.

"I can guarantee you I don't swim like one."

A round of chuckles rumbled from the descendants.

Was I seriously bathing with four guys? What had possessed me to agree to such a thing? I was in over my head. "You guys think that's funny, huh?" I cupped my hands and tossed water into each of their faces.

For a stunned moment, they stared at me, and then I was sailing through the air. Kieran, who was the closest, had picked me up and tossed me to Zade.

Oh dear God. What have I done?

Zade, in turn, flung me to Issik, who launched me to Jase. Before he could pass me back to Kieran, I wound my arms around his neck. "No more," I warned, pushing his firm chest playfully. "You're making me dizzy."

Jase grinned at me, his eyes sparkling like the rascal that he was, but the glimmer swiftly shifted to something else as we both remembered our near nakedness. I should have loosened my fingers and floated away from him, back into neutral territory, but I didn't. None of us had discussed the other part of the bond. They could feel my emotions, but also we had an attraction between us. I didn't know how to handle it.

Was it okay that I wanted to kiss Jase, or would the others get jealous?

Was it okay that I wanted to kiss them all?

Did I even have a choice in the matter?

I acted on instinct, hoping it wouldn't steer me wrong. My arms tightened around Jase's neck, bringing his face closer to mine. The water lapped in a rhythmic motion against us, and I could feel his breath against my lips. "Don't you dare think about blowing any tranquility in my direction."

His smile returned, heartbreaking in its beauty. "I wouldn't dream of it. Now, are you going to kiss me?"

My head angled to the left, aligning our mouths. "I haven't made up my mind yet." I could sense the eyes of the others on us, and my blood raced.

I had no intention of playing favorites, but Jase was right here, tempting me with his dimples. His arms came to the sides of my hips, as the warm water licked over my breasts. The bra I had on offered very little coverage. Those violet eyes enthralled me, and everything else ceased to exist when Jase gazed at me. I didn't give myself the chance to think.

This was what I wanted.

This was what I'd dreamed about.

On the next wave, I pressed my lips to his and was met with resistance, as if he hadn't believed I would actually kiss him. But in the next breath, his will crumbled. His fingers dove into my hair, keeping my mouth to his, and my mind became filled with nothing but the taste and scent of Jase. I wrapped my legs around his waist, pressing our bodies together. The back of his knuckles stroked my cheek like velvet, and I deepened the kiss, needing more of him. My fingers played with the wet curls at the nape of his neck. I couldn't stop touching him. Stop kissing him. I was swimming in lust.

Parting my lips, I purred at the feeling of his tongue grazing against mine. I breathed his breath. How far was I willing to go? In the heat of the moment, I would have killed him if he stopped kissing me. So when his lips went lax against mine, I growled, wondering what I had done wrong. My lashes fluttered open, and I expected to see Jase's vibrant eyes gleaming at me. But they were still closed, and the arms that had been around me fell flaccidly to his sides. Trepidation reared its ugly head inside me.

"Jase?"

He didn't move, and his body was slowly sinking. Memories of Jase being attacked and falling into the lake rose up inside me, bringing panic with it.

"This isn't funny. Cut the crap."

Nothing. No twitching smirk. No dimples. No smart comebacks. In my arms, his body was lifeless and heavy, even with the help of the water.

What had I done to him? I racked my brain. We had only kissed. How could that render him unconscious? It was a question that would have to wait for an answer.

"Jase!" I yelled, shaking his shoulders.

As I shrieked, the other descendants surrounded me. They took one look at me then at Jase.

"What happened?" Issik demanded in a tone frosty enough to freeze over the basin.

"I-I don't know," I stammered, letting Zade take Jase out of my arms. The warm water suddenly felt frigid. "We were just… and then he went limp. What did I do?"

Snickers erupted from the three of them, and it took me a heartbeat to figure out what they found so entertaining. This was a life or death situation. I made one little comment about Jase being limp, and they got all childish on me.

"Grow up. That's not what I meant. How can you guys joke at a time like this?" I snapped.

Zade's brows rose as he pulled Jase's body to the edge of the basin. "I think you're forgetting one very important detail."

Kicking off in the water, I swam alongside Issik and

Kieran. "What?" I urged him, feeling confused and scared for Jase.

"You were kissing," Kieran answered.

My gaze swung to the poison dragon, waiting for him to elaborate. "I fail to see how that is important." I knew the others were watching. That had been part of the appeal, but looking back, what had I been thinking? I didn't know what I was doing with these four guys. That was becoming quite clear.

"Maybe she kissed him to death," Issik offered, jumping out of the water to help Zade lift Jase out of it.

"Funny." Then I reconsidered it. "Wait. That's not possible, is it?"

Issik stood at the edge with his hands extended to pull me up. "Let's hope not."

I placed my hands in his, and Issik raised me out of the water like I weighed nothing. "Is he going to be okay?"

"Jase? Definitely. It is going to take a lot more than a kiss to get rid of this stubborn bastard." Issik handed me a towel before wrapping one around his lower half. I'd completely forgotten about our lack of clothing.

Securing the towel under my arms, I ran my eyes ran over Jase. He looked like he was sleeping peacefully, his chest rising and falling in an even pattern. *At least he is breathing.* I plucked a towel from a bamboo shelf and draped it over Jase's lower half.

Zade inspected Jase, beads of water dripping off his golden chest, before being caught by the cloth around his hips. "There doesn't seem to be anything wrong with him physically." His gaze slid to me.

"Why are you staring at me like I murdered your best friend?" He was being a little melodramatic. Zade's glare wasn't quite an accusation, but something made him suspicious of me.

"Damn," Zade cursed, forking a hand through his dark, wet hair. "We should have seen this coming."

My fingers clasped together. "Are you going to tell me what is going on?"

Zade grimaced. "We need to teach you how to harness your tranquility ability, or we all might be dozing."

I stared at Zade, taking in what he had said. *Tranquility*. It had been days since I found the stone and in return absorbed its power, but I hadn't thought much about it since. Apparently, I should have been more concerned with my newfound ability to breathe tranquility, because if I understood what Zade was saying, I had put Jase into a deep slumber.

Taking a step away from Jase, I shook my head. "I did this?"

"I'm afraid so, Little Gem," Zade replied in sympathy.

My bad ankle gave out on me, but Issik kept me on my feet. His hands grabbed either side of my arms, pulling me against his chest. My belly sunk. I was horrified. I couldn't believe I had done that without even knowing. Until I figured out how to control this power inside me, I wouldn't be kissing anyone. I was dangerous.

Kieran patted me on the back. "This is a first. You put the tranquility dragon to sleep. Priceless."

"What can I say? I can do the impossible."

"Don't despair," Issik whispered in my ear, feeling the

gush of sadness inside me. "We could all use some sleep. It's been a long day."

I nodded. Words were unable to pass through the lump in my throat.

"You'll learn to control it. We all have," Kieran assured me, but it didn't do much to ease my distress.

Issik started to steer me out of the room. "Wait." I dug in the heel of my good foot, and Issik looked down at me with cool blue eyes. "We're not going to leave him here, are we?"

Issik glanced over his shoulder to where Jase still lay on the stone ground. Zade hovered over him. "Zade will make sure he is comfortable."

"Why don't I believe you?"

"It's not every day we get the opportunity to pull one over on Jase. We should be thanking you," Kieran added over my shoulder.

A practical joke? How could they conceive of such a thing right now? Sometimes they made me want to bang my head against the nearest wall.

Too tired to argue, I let Kieran and Issik lead me out of the shower room, and up the winding staircase. The curves reminded me of the snake curled around the outside of the castle, and I wouldn't be surprised if the layout mirrored the twining stone serpent's location. Kieran and I might need to have a talk about his choice of décor. Snakes were downright disgusting, but the inside of the keep redeemed itself. It was plush and a gardener's wet dream. Every corner had plants or flowers in it. Issik ducked under a vine hanging from an archway.

The most disturbing thought entered my mind as I watched him. What kind of critters lived in the vines and the plants? They were all over the castle. "Hot Lips, what is with the snake theme?"

Kieran didn't blink at his nickname. They'd gotten used to the names I'd given them. "Are you afraid of reptiles?"

Dumb question. "Snakes, spiders, bugs, all the usual creepy-crawly shit."

Issik smirked... well, a smirk for Issik meant his lips barely moved. "Just put them to sleep."

Kieran chuckled, and my hand automatically smacked him in the chest. The poisonous dragon frowned at me.

"Nervous tic." I smiled sweetly.

No one bought that excuse, but we had come to a door, and Kieran pushed it open, sweeping his arms in a welcoming gesture. "Your chambers await. Bug free, of course."

I walked into the room, looking around. "You swear? I don't want to wake up staring at an eight-legged freak." The bed in the center of the room was supported by bamboo stalks and covered in a soft sage duvet. Its cozy exterior beckoned me.

Kieran strutted into the room, drawing the curtains closed at the window. The room was submerged in darkness. "If you have any unexpected visitors, just yell. We won't be far away." He grabbed a clean shirt from one of the drawers, and slipped it over my head.

Pushing my arms through the sleeves, the towel fell to the floor. I padded across the floor and climbed onto the bed. "Where will you be..." My words got cut off as Issik dropped his towel to throw on a pair of nylon shorts, giving me a view of his butt. I swallowed. "...staying?"

"I'll be in the room next to yours, and Zade will be in the other," Issik answered me, completely oblivious of my jaw still on the ground.

"Maybe one of us should stay with her. If Tianna..." I locked eyes with Kieran.

He didn't need to finish the thought. We all knew what would happen if the witch showed up. T-R-O-U-B-L-E. That's what. Like the kind that would get me killed, thus getting the descendants killed. None of us wanted to die.

"We could take shifts. Rotate each night," Kieran proposed.

Did I get a say in this? How did I feel about having one of them sleep in the same room with me?

Hot.

Bothered.

And worried—what if I accidentally breathed on one of them in my sleep? The descendants would be no help to me if I constantly put them in a deep slumber. "I'm not sure that is a good idea."

Kieran arched his pierced brow, pushing his damp hair away from his face. He looked different without the spikes, but still handsome. "Two against one. You're overruled."

My head hit the pillow. "You guys are lucky I'm too tired to argue."

Issik came up to the edge of the bed, tucking the covers in around me. "We can discuss it in the morning." He turned to Kieran. "I'll stay tonight."

Snuggling deeper into the bed, I waited for Kieran to

protest. It would be like them to start fighting over who got to spend the night, but he surprised me.

Leaning over the bed, Kieran pressed a gentle kiss to my forehead. "Sleep tight, Blondie. Don't let the bed bugs bite." His lips curled against my skin.

My fingers gripped onto the blanket tighter. "I should breathe on you," I uttered without heat behind the words. I listened to Kieran's feet clatter over the floor as he left, probably smiling to himself the entire way, the damn devil.

I searched the darkness for Issik and spotted him in the corner, settling into a chair. Shadows danced across his face, giving him an aura of danger. "Are you planning on sleeping in the chair?"

"I've slept in far worse places. There's no need to worry about me."

But I did worry about him, and after the day we'd had, he deserved something better than being scrunched into a rickety chair in the corner. I fidgeted on the bed for another minute before I gave in and glared at him.

"This is ridiculous. I can't sleep knowing you're over there. The bed is big enough for us both." And I wanted him close, but not close enough I could unintentionally knock him out for good. I patted the bed beside me. "What are you waiting for?"

His long legs stretched out in front of him so that his toes almost touched the bedframe. "I'm deciding if it's a good idea for me to be close to you."

"Because of my tranquility?"

He shook his head. "Something like that wouldn't keep me from you."

The way he said those words—so possessive—had my pulse racing.

"I'm not sure I trust myself to sleep next to you."

"You did it before," I reminded him.

"And I didn't get much sleep," he stated dryly.

"Fine," I grumbled. "Be a stubborn, uncomfortable mule." I closed my eyes, telling myself to forget about Issik. I lasted less than five minutes. My eyes popped open to find Issik's gaze on me. In the dark, his light blue irises popped. "If I'm going to get any sleep tonight, you can't sit there staring at me."

"And if you keep talking, neither of us is going to sleep," he countered. Silence greeted us both as we engaged in an epic stare-down. Issik finally gave in, and inside, I squealed like a little girl at the candy shop.

He rose from the chair to walk around to the other side of the bed. The mattress dipped under his weight, making it so I rolled toward the center of the bed. Our arms were side by side when he lay down, and we both stared up at the ceiling. I angled my head to the side, checking to see if his eyes were closed.

He peeked at me from under half-lidded lashes. "Happy now?"

I grinned, snuggling deep into the blanket and closing my eyes. "Very."

He let out a long exhale.

As I was about to drop off into deep sleep, Issik's husky voice pulled me back from the edge of a dream. It had been a really good dream too. "So I guess you like Jase."

My shoulders moved in an unseen shrug. "I guess, but I like you too." My eyes lifted to his, gauging his reaction.

Like most things with Issik, it was hard to see what he was thinking. "We've never shared a girl before."

I understood how he felt. Unsure. Curious. And maybe even a little scared. "Me neither," I replied.

His lips twitched.

"That's not what I meant." I bumped my shoulder into his. "I've never had feelings for more than one person at a time before. Let alone four, but I can't choose between you. I won't." It was important I made that clear now.

"Haven't you already?"

Did I detect a hint of disappointment? Where was this coming from? I took a stab in the dark. "Why? Because you haven't kissed me? Not that it matters now. You couldn't kiss me even if you wanted to."

"Tranquility wouldn't keep me from kissing you," he answered calmly, ensnaring me with his cool gaze.

There went my heart, bumping in my chest. "You guys are going to drive me crazy."

A smile cracked his serious demeanor. "Now you know how we feel." Issik leaned over and kissed the tip of my nose. His wintery breath washed over my face, tickling my lips. "Goodnight, Little Warrior."

Now I understood what he meant about not getting any sleep. The scent of him teased my senses until late into the night, following me into my dreams.

When I woke, my world was washed in green, and my mind was muddled. A hundred different shades collided around me. Through the sheer curtains, beams of sunlight streamed across the floor. As I blinked, it all hit me at once.

Oh yes, Kieran.

I'd been whisked off to Viperus.

Just as I'd become somewhat familiar with Wakeland Keep, they threw me into another castle with as many corridors, stairs, and rooms. I was back at square one. And to make things more complicated than they already were, I had this ability I didn't know how to deal with or control.

Sighing, I felt something pinning my belly to the bed. Glancing down, I saw a muscular arm draped over me, and my heart swelled. Coolness radiated from the ice dragon, who in sleep looked less menacing and softer. I reached out, brushing a lock of blond hair off the side of his sharp cheek.

If I knew the descendants, today would be another long day. We had a stone to find, so I took these few precious moments of peace, to study the dragon who guarded his heart fiercely. He wasn't one to open up, but Issik made me want to be the one who melted the ice he surrounded himself with so fiercely.

I couldn't think of a better face to wake up to, and a smile spread over my lips. Our legs had intertwined during the night, and Issik must have some crazy leg hair because it tickled my thigh. Tilting my head down to look, I saw a bug the size of a Snickers bar scampering across my leg. I kicked as hard as I could, screaming. Long. Loud. And piercing. It sounded as if I was being held at gunpoint.

I was going to kill Kieran and his jungle.

If the bug didn't eat me first.

Issik jumped up, dragon scales peppering his torso. No sooner had he sat up than I was scrambling into his lap. The safest place to be during an invasion of critters was on higher ground.

"What's wrong? Where is she?" His frosty eyes glowed while his arms secured me against his chest.

I pointed my finger at the end of the bed, my bravery no bigger than a teaspoon at the moment. "There. I-it was a bug." I waited for him to kick into exterminator mode, but he just sat there, staring at my face.

"A bug?" he echoed. "Are you telling me that you woke me from a dead sleep, screaming at the top of your lungs, for a bug?"

"Shit. We don't have bugs like that in Illinois."

The door to my room burst open, and a shirtless Zade dominated the doorway. "What happened? Are you hurt? Did Tianna—" His voice cut off when he saw me situated in Issik's lap.

I groaned, dropping my forehead onto Issik's shoulder, who ran a hand through his hair.

"It was a bug," he told Zade.

The Golden God leaned a shoulder against the door, eyeing me with amusement. "I warned you there are bugs."

"You could have told me that they are as big as my hand!"

"This was more fun."

And there went my good mood. "I need coffee," I grumbled, removing myself from atop Issik.

That was twice I'd landed in ice prince's lap in less than twenty-four hours. It was twice I'd slept with him in the same bed, and yet, he was the only one who hadn't kissed me. Why did that bother me?

A fresh pot of steaming coffee waited downstairs in the kitchen for me. Alice was my favorite person in the world. Along with the caffeine kick were pancakes... and Jase, already on what appeared to be his second stack. His jet black hair was messy from sleep, and he turned those violet eyes on me as we walked into the room.

"How did you sleep last night?" Zade asked, razzing Jase.

Jase swallowed a mouthful of food, his eyes narrowing on Zade and Issik. "What the hell happened?"

Zade looked at me with a stupid grin on his face, while and Issik's lips twitched. Kieran chose that moment to walk into the room. "Did I miss it?"

"Olivia?" Jase called to me. "Do you want to tell me what these idiots are talking about?"

"Hmm," I replied, plucking a piece of fruit from the bowl on the counter, and shoving it in my mouth. If I was stuffing my face, then I didn't have to admit what I had done. "Not really," I confessed.

Setting his fork down, he folded his hands on the table. "I'm waiting."

My eyes darted around the table, looking at the others for help. They were useless. Taking my cup of coffee, I sat down at the table next to him. Giving him my "remember I'm just a girl" and "this isn't my fault" look, I told him what happened. "I might have accidentally put you to sleep when we kissed."

Jase didn't move a muscle. "You're joking."

"I wish I was," I muttered, taking a sip of coffee.

His eyes darkened, flickering around the table at Kieran, Zade, and Issik, who were all doubled over with silent laughter. I wished I had longer legs so I could kick each one of them in the shin from here.

"I'll deal with the three of you later." Leaning back in his chair, Jase focused back on me. "We're going to need to move up those lessons I had planned, it seems, but not today. Do you think you could avoid knocking any of us out for one day?"

"As long as none of you try to kiss me," I snapped back at him.

A sardonic twist spread over his lips. "Fair enough."

The table erupted in groans of complaint from everyone but Jase and me.

Jase picked his fork up to resume tackling his food, but

first, he gave the others a lecture. "I'm trusting you guys can keep your lips off her for a few days. We can't afford to have anyone sleeping on the job, not when we're so close. Olivia needs all the protection we can give her. There is no room for mistakes."

We passed the food around and piled it on our plates. To an outsider, it would have appeared that everyone had ignored Jase, but that wasn't the case. They had heard him. They just chose not to comment. For one, it would piss off Jase to get no responses. And secondly, food was in front of them. Jase should have known better than to have tried to reason with them when food was involved.

I sank into my chair, nursing my coffee and assessing how I was feeling about the no kissing rule. It made perfect sense, but then why was I so put out about it?

My day didn't get much better.

As expected, after breakfast, Jase went into commander mode, barking orders, and then the five of us were back in the woods. It all happened so fast. One minute I was grabbing my second cup of coffee, and the next, I was ushered outside, barely awake and functioning. I didn't even know what the game plan was.

Throwing my blonde hair into a messy bun, I glanced up at the sun beating down on us. "Where are we going?" I whined.

Kieran startled me, suddenly appearing at my side. I'd been concentrating on the ground, looking for hidden holes. "These woods are filled with tombs and burial grounds of our people. It might be a good place to search for the stone."

Graves? Not the first hiding place that came to my

mind. And honestly, I wasn't looking forward to disturbing the resting place of the dead. Talk about bad mojo. A witch had already cursed them. Pissing off a bunch of ghosts did not sound like a great idea. But what did I know?

"Are you guys trying to get me to fall through the world again?" My eyes continued staring hard at the ground in front of me. The last thing I needed was to twist my other ankle.

Speaking of which, my injured one was feeling much better. The pressure of my weight didn't seem to bother it. My explanation: one of my dragons had done something to speed up the healing process.

Kieran lifted a branch out of my way, waiting for me to pass under it. "How many times do I have to apologize?"

Mischief lit up my eyes. "How about a kiss instead?"

Zade and Jase laughed. I even got a chuckle out of Issik. Glad they found me so humorous, but it was Kieran's slow smile that dazzled me. Surrounded in miles and miles of dense woods, Kieran had never looked more in his element; he'd never looked more attractive to me.

"Don't tempt me."

They were the ones tempting me. "When do the dragons get to come out?" I asked, thinking this would go a lot faster on a dragon's back.

Kieran shook his head, a smile tugging at his lips. "You're going to be very distracting."

"I could be annoying or boring instead," I offered.

His fingers brushed the loose strands of hair sticking to the back of my neck. "No, I think I prefer distracting."

A shiver danced down my spine, taking on a whole new meaning when a shrill vibrated through the woods. The sound was followed by two dark shadows flying over the towering pines. Their wings weren't quite as large as a dragon's, but they were still impressive in size.

"You might get your wish," Jase rumbled, his eyes glowing.

I knew what that look meant. He was about to shift.

In seconds, silvery purple scales papered Jase's entire body as his muscles and bones expanded. The end result was a pissed off dragon. His form was too large for the forest, and trees bent and crunched under his weight. Throwing back his angular head, he let out a roar from deep within his chest into the sky.

In answer, the squawking noise sounded again, and my elation at seeing Jase's dragon was overshadowed by the things circling overhead.

"Griffins," Zade hissed.

Oh, hell to the no.

I was definitely not a fan of the large flying birds with the legs of a lion and a serpent's tail.

"Stay with her," Issik instructed Zade and Kieran, who sandwiched me between their firm shoulders.

And then the viking ripped off his shirt, shifting into a fierce dragon with white and blue scales that looked like an ice storm—jagged and wicked. Kicking off his hind legs, Issik took to the sky, unfazed by the tree branches whipping him.

My arms wrapped around myself. "Does this mean Tianna has found us already?" I asked in a small voice.

Kieran's gaze zeroed in on the griffins. "I'm afraid so, Blondie."

"That was fast," I muttered to myself.

Craning my neck upward, I searched the sky. On the ground, under the thick foliage, it was hard to see what was happening. Then, of course, there came two giant men towering over me. I understood it was for my own safety, but it made keeping track of my other two dragons difficult. How was I to know if they were hurt?

"They'll be fine," Zade assured, reading the concern that had soured my expression.

I glared sideways at him. "I thought your emotion was anger."

A ghost of a smile appeared on his lips. "It is, but I don't need to feel your emotions to know you're worried. It is all there in your face."

Kieran breathed hard, vengeance shining in his eyes, which were a startling shade of emerald. "Tianna might send her goons to keep track of us, but they're no match for Issik and Jase."

I could sense his desire to shift and the resolve it took to stay in his human form. "I don't understand her. She wants the stones, wants their power, and yet, she is making it damn near impossible for me to find them."

Zade shook his head. "It is a waste of time to try and get inside the head of a witch."

Our discussion was interrupted, when something rammed into a tree off to our left. I whipped toward the direction of the splintering wood. Jase had slammed one of the griffins into a tree, and had its wing pinned with his claw. Feathers drifted down from the branches, while the beast shrieked, pecking at Jase with his large beak.

I was about to take action when Issik and the other griffin hit the ground like an earthquake. Grass and rocks trembled under my feet. Kieran caught my elbow to steady me as I lost my balance from the impact. My palms flattened on his chest.

Rendered immobile, I stood curled against Kieran and watched Issik fight the griffin. His jaws snapped like thunder cracking in the sky. More feathers coated the ground in a mangled mess. The griffin scored Issik's underbelly with its claws, and the dragon reared its head, letting out a roar of anger and pain.

I jerked into motion, running toward Issik, but Kieran and Zade were there to stop me before I made it two feet. Kieran wrapped his arms around my waist, pulling my back against his chest. "It's safer if you stay with us," he murmured in my ear.

Frantically, I flung my gaze back to Issik. *Is he okay? Had the griffin hurt him more?* My heart thrashed in my chest. I couldn't lose him. Any of them. Not now.

It turned out I had worked myself into a tizzy for nothing. As my eyes landed on Issik and the griffin, Issik opened his large jaw and wrapped his teeth around the griffin's neck. Jerking his head in one quick movement, he ripped the head from the creature's body. The ice dragon tossed his long neck, releasing the feathery head. It rolled on the ground before coming to a stop. A splattered trail of blood painted the earth.

I tried not to gag at the gruesome sight.

Burying my face in Kieran's chest, I turned away. His

arms came around me, keeping me close. "Don't weep for her spies," he murmured, brushing his lips through my hair.

If Kieran had been Jase, he would sense it wasn't sadness or pity I felt, but fear. Peeking through my curtain of tangled and loose strands of hair, I saw Issik watched me with intense eyes. My actions might have seemed as if what he had done revolted me, which in a way it had, but it wasn't Issik I was disgusted with. He had done what needed to be done to keep us safe. I didn't fault him for that. If anyone was to blame, it was Tianna.

I projected my thoughts toward him, remembering he could hear me. *"Are you okay?"*

The ice dragon's angular head gave a curt nod. *"I didn't mean to frighten you."*

I took a step forward, but Kieran didn't let me go far. One more griffin remained. I huffed. *"I was taken by surprise. I'm not afraid of you,"* I assured him.

The beating of wings flapping in the air reached my ears. Jase hovered over us, a griffin clenched in his claws. Releasing it from his clutches, the beast fell to the ground. Zade stood over the creature and pounced, grabbing it around the neck. "She's ours," he growled at the griffin. "Take that back to your witch."

Damn straight I was.

Then he pitched the creature aside like it was worthless. The beast whimpered as it rolled on the ground, eventually coming up on its feet. It gave one long caw and pushed off the ground with its hind legs, taking to the sky. The descendants let him go to deliver a warning to Tianna.

Another crisis averted, but there was no time to rest. Tianna knew where we were, which would make finding the Star that much harder.

Jase and Issik shifted out of their dragon forms, giving me a nice view of their firm tushes, and I tried to remind my hormones that now were not the time to get excited. We had just escaped one of Tianna's famous attacks. I needed to focus.

The descendants had come prepared for the unexpected dragon shifts. Kieran tossed Issik and Jase clothes from the backpack he'd brought along. Issik was about to slip on a T-shirt when he turned around and faced me. Winter swirled in his harsh steel eyes. A red cut slashed across his chest from his right shoulder to his left hip. It was raw and beaded with blood.

A sharp inhale burned my lungs. "You're hurt," I whispered, moving toward him as I remembered the griffin clawing him. My hand extended, but I didn't touch him for fear of causing him more pain. "And don't tell me it's just a scratch."

Issik kept his gaze on mine, even when his fingers wrapped around my wrist, bringing my hand to his heart. "Well, it is. Griffin claws are sharp, but they won't kill me."

"I'd hug you, but I don't want to get blood on my shirt."

He smirked. "Good thing I don't care about your shirt." In the next breath, I was engulfed in his cool arms. And he was right: I didn't give a damn about my shirt.

He was alive. That was all that really mattered.

And finding the Star of Poison, of course.

One might think after an attack by a pair of griffins, we'd call it a day, and head back to Viperus Keep. Nope. Not Jase.

We pushed on, heading to one of the burial grounds.

Yippee.

I waded through the brush, pushing aside branches and swatting at bugs. "Remind me again whose genius idea it was to go traipsing around the woods midday?" This seemed to be the question on everyone's mind. An added bonus was it annoyed Jase.

"Jase," Issik, Zade, and Kieran groaned in unison.

"Do you want to break this curse or not?" Jase countered in his defense. "The Star of Poison is out here... somewhere."

"It might be easier to find a unicorn or the pot of gold at the end of a rainbow." My tone was naturally sarcastic —all part of my charm. The descendants loved me for it.

Kieran took a pause to wipe the sweat off his brow

J.L WEIL

with the back of his hand. Zade and Issik continued walking a few paces up ahead of us.

"Why is it so hot today? It's not like we're in volcano country," I complained.

Despite the thin material of my clothes, everything stuck to my skin, including dirt, bugs, leaves, and anything else I managed to come into contact with then. "I'd trade my right arm for a pool right now."

"There will be no loss of appendages," Jase added sternly.

"Geez, Dimples, I didn't mean it literally."

"The sun is brutal today. Unusually so," Kieran admitted, glancing up through the green canopy of leaves. It offered little protection from the blazing sun. "Viperus is never this hot."

"Something is messing with the isles' climate," Jase concluded.

There were two things I could think of that might be responsible, Tianna or the stones. They were the only items on the isles that had the power to do something like this.

A scowl creased Kieran's brow. It was rare to the see the carefree dragon frowning. "It has to be the curse."

Jase nodded. "My thoughts exactly. We need to find the next stone sooner rather than later. I have a feeling things are going to get more complicated, if you know what I mean." He peered at Kieran over my head, sharing a look.

I raised my hand, wondering if it was a good idea to be doing that while walking, but it was too late. The deed

64

was done. "No, I don't know what you mean. Can one of you explain?"

"Put your hand down," Jase ordered. "You're going to trip over something and break a bone."

Kieran flashed me a grin. "Don't worry, I'll catch you."

"There is no way in hell I'm going to trip," I proudly defended, tipping my chin up. "You guys act like I can't walk and chew gum at the same time." The truth was I probably couldn't, but that was beside the point. "I can walk with both my freaking arms in the air if I want to, thank you very much." I proceeded to show them how awesome my coordination was. "I'm far too poised to—" Then I tripped... over a tombstone nonetheless.

Really? What are the chances?

I miraculously stayed on my feet, but it was instinct for the descendants to save me. Kieran's hand stabilized my elbow, and I couldn't remember if it had been there before or after I tripped.

"You were saying?" Kieran asked, grinning like the devil himself.

I blew the hair out of my face and glowered at him. "Well, who the hell put a gravestone right in the middle of the path?"

The others gathered around. "Let's spread out, cover more ground."

Kieran shadowed my movements, and I assumed he was assigned Olivia babysitting detail, not that I minded. The only things we were going to find here were spirits wanting to possess my body, or talk to me from the other side. I'd had enough of ghosts. No need to encourage more.

"Do you sense anything?" Kieran asked, leaning close to me and whispering in my ear.

I stopped in my tracks and glanced over at him. "I'm not a stone detector. There isn't an internal beacon in me that sends an alert if there is a magical dragon crystal nearby."

Kieran straightened up, rubbing a hand over the back of his neck while pondering me. I tended to confuse the dragon descendants. It was obvious they'd never dealt with a girl from the city. Or I could be extra unique. "It doesn't hurt to try. Who knows what you're capable of? Did you ever think you'd be able to render people unconscious by breathing on them?"

"Uh, no."

"There you go." Kieran put his hands on my shoulders and steered me to the center of the misty graveyard. Carved stones were embedded in the green grass all around me. "Now close your eyes."

"This is never going to work," I stated, crossing my arms over my chest. My flimsy shirt was nearly see-through from sweat, but I couldn't have cared less. They had seen me naked before.

"We won't know unless you try. Now stop being stubborn and concentrate," he insisted.

"On what? I don't know what I'm supposed to be focusing on."

Kieran heaved a heavy groan. "Olivia, close your eyes. Envision a stone just like the one you found but emerald in color."

"That's not how this works," I told him. At least I was pretty sure it wasn't.

"Olivia," he warned me.

This was stupid, but the only way I would get him off my back was to do what he suggested, no matter how silly it seemed. Shifting my weight to one side, I let my eyes drift shut. Leaves rustled in the air with a gentle breeze that did nothing to relieve the heat. As I continued to listen, waiting for something fucking spectacular to happen, my mind wandered.

I wonder what Alice is making for dinner. Suddenly, I was famished.

Is that a wolf howling?

Are there wolves in the Veil? It's probably something way worse.

Then I got a whiff of Kieran and that was it. My concentration was shot to hell. I found myself leaning in toward the smell, drawn to him like a magnet. I had a beacon all right—a beacon for the descendants.

Kieran must have felt it as well. His body brushed up against mine, and I sunk into him. "What do you feel?"

My cheeks flamed. "You don't want to know."

The warmth of his chuckle breezed through my hair. "What am I going to do with you?"

I could think of a few things.

"Are you focusing?"

On the sound of your deep, husky voice, I thought, but he probably didn't want to hear that. Or did he? My eyes fluttered open after feeling absolutely nothing but the tingling awareness of Kieran's proximity. I turned to face him. He watched me with keen interest in his bright eyes. Nibbling on my lower lip, I savored his intense stare and soft mouth. The air was charged between us and had me wanting nothing more than to press my lips to his.

But I couldn't.

Kieran must have forgotten about my little ability to put people to sleep because he leaned forward, his passion pulling him to me like a baited fish. I opened my mouth to stop him, but Kieran swooped in, taking possession of my lips.

My hands steadied me on his chest while I struggled to control myself, but the need to melt into the sweet sensations he offered overwhelmed all my rational thoughts. The cool metal of his lip ring slid smoothly over my tender lips. I sighed.

And that was all it took to remind me what my breath could do.

I shoved at his pecs. "Kieran. You can't kiss me."

He blinked, staring down at me with heavy, half-lidded eyes. "Why? Because we might get caught making out on the job? Don't worry about Jase. I can handle him."

I snorted, shaking my head. "I'm not worried about Jase. I don't want to have to catch your massive body when I accidentally knock you out."

"It wouldn't be the first time I've been exposed to tranquility. I can't tell you the number of times Jase has hit me with his sleeping vapors."

"That explains a lot," I retorted, but my feisty tone went right over his Mohawk head.

Kieran took a step back from me. "Did you get anything before you decided to kiss me?"

A short puff escaped my lips. "First off, you kissed me. And secondly, I told you it wouldn't work."

"Or maybe you didn't try."

"Don't you think I want to find the stone?" Each word I filled with sharpness.

"I don't know what you want."

My arms flew up in the air. "You are impossible." I stalked away from Kieran to search out a descendant with half a brain. Zade found me first.

He strode beside me, bringing a wave of heat with him, not that I needed more. "Did you find anything?" he asked with hope shimmering in his cinnamon eyes.

My hands landed on my hips, and I narrowed my eyes as I scanned the sacred ground. "Only a bunch of graves and an imbecile."

Zade lifted a brow, giving me a funny expression.

"Don't ask. Can we go home now?" I'd had enough stone searching for the day.

His lips quirked. "You're definitely talking about Kieran."

"I'll never understand the four of you."

"That probably makes us even."

He might have had a point.

I nearly jumped for joy, when Jase and Issik found us a few minutes later to call it a day. If I never had to hike through the woods again, I would die a happy camper. I knew the likelihood of that actually happening was low, but a girl could dream. Days like today made the task of finding the stones seem impossible. We needed something to point us in the right direction.

I needed to fall down another hole, and have a chat with a spirit. They seemed to be partial to appearing in water. Why was that?

The walk back was quiet. Zade ended up carrying me most of the way. My little legs had given up on me. With my head resting on his strong shoulder, we reached the castle as the last slivers of dusk disappeared behind the trees.

It was hard to not let disappointment color my mood, even after a hot meal from Alice, the goddess of the kitchen. Unlike last night, I didn't suggest a group shower. I'd learned my lesson. The descendants were more than I could deal with all at once.

As I headed up the stairs to my room, my head continued to fill with negativity and defeat, but one smile from a dragon shifter at the top of the landing had the ability to turn my frown upside down.

Jase's fingers slipped under my chin, tilting my face upward to meet his gaze. "Why do you look like you lost your best friend?"

My shoulders fell, relaxing in his presence. "Sorry. Having a bad day."

He weaved his fingers with mine, leading me down the hall. "Compared to some of your other days, today wasn't half bad."

Maybe, but that didn't mean it still didn't suck some serious ass.

When we got to my room, the other three dragons were hanging out in front of my door. Breezing past them, I ditched my shoes and let down my hair, shaking it out. "So who's staying tonight?" I asked, spinning around to face the four descendants.

Everyone volunteered at once, including Issik, who had already had a turn. I should have known better than to open this can of worms. It would have been less complicated if I had picked one to stay, but I couldn't do that either. We needed a system, or I could count on fights breaking out each night before bed, which was the last thing I needed—more chaos.

They all talked over each other, and their voices were growing louder. It was only a matter of time before the chest bumping and fist flying started.

Standing in the middle of the room with my arms crossed, I tapped my foot, trying to decide which one I would punch in the dick first. How else would I get them to stop being complete animals? They were lucky I liked them... sometimes. I wanted to knock their heads together, but I was too damn tired to get physical with them.

"Hey!" I bellowed, my voice carrying out the door and down the corridor. "Enough!"

Four muscular men froze with their firsts in midair.

"If you guys need to beat the shit out of each other to figure out who is staying, take it downstairs. I'm going to bed."

I didn't wait for a response. I gave them my back, and went to the bamboo dresser in the corner of the room. Flipping my shirt over my head, I dug through the top drawer, pulling out an oversized T-shirt, and tugged it on. I wiggled out of my pants, leaving them where they fell.

The silence I was appreciating erupted into dragon chaos once again.

Gah!

Rolling my eyes, I shuffled barefoot across the textured wood floors as I ignored the quartet. I climbed into bed, let my exhausted bones sink into the padding, and closed my eyes, coaxing my mind to sleep with the deep voices of Issik, Jase, Kieran, and Zade storming around me. It was hard, considering the stress of the last few days, and the loud arguing, but whether it was exhaustion or something else, my dreams pulled me under.

The streets of Chicago blurred as I came to the Veil, flying on a dragon, and of course, the witch was there. Tianna's face rose through the haze of images, becoming clearer as I fell deeper into my subconscious. She'd found a way to get to me where the descendants couldn't protect me.

Fucking bitch.

She stood inside an elaborate iron gate, her deep red hair blowing in the wind. "You can't run forever."

I put on my best impression of being as bored as rocks. "Who says I'm running?"

Her blood red lips curled. "Isn't that what you do? Run away?"

My toes dug into the dirt. "Don't pretend like you know anything about me."

Her hips swayed, in a sexiness I could never emulate while she sauntered toward me. "I know how much you care for the dragon descendants. I know how far you're willing to go to save them."

"I know a few things too. I know you're a bitch. I know you

can't get the power you desire unless I find the stones. How's that working out for you?" I asked with a smug grin.

Her creamy hand flew in the air to strike me, but it stopped just shy of my left cheek. The sudden display of rage caught me off guard. I flinched. It looked as if someone had a bit of a temper simmering under the surface. Her eyes harbored flames of hate. "Watch what you say to me. My patience can be... prickly at times. I can make things very difficult for you, Olivia."

I shuddered at the way my name rolled of her lips. Hadn't she already been doing that? This time, I kept my trap shut, not brave enough to push the witch and her wrath. "What do you want from me? What is the point of you invading my sleep?"

Her red nails skimmed across her equally bold lip color. "I like that you're a get-to-the-point kind of girl. It makes our relationship less complicated. I want the stones. I thought that was clear. Time is running out, so I'm here to give you a gentle nudge."

I snorted. "A nudge? What do you think I've been doing? Knitting a blanket?"

"Just remember I'll be around to whisper in your ear, and give you a snippet of motivation from time to time."

That sounded ominous. I didn't like it. Not. One. Single. Bit.

I was about to tell her what she could do with her threat when a sudden pecking noise broke through my slumber, severing the dream. It sounded like someone was throwing rocks at my window. My first thought, it was one of the descendants trying to be cute, but would they go outside when I slept right next door? It didn't make sense, especially when one of them was sleeping beside me. I blinked, turning my head to see which one it was. Kieran had curled up next to me.

Slipping out of bed, I padded over to the window and peeked down into the courtyard below. A woman in a pale dress stood at the base of the castle—directly below my room. Her skin had an iridescent glow about it almost as if she was transparent. I was positive if I had been in reach and touched her, my hand would have passed right through her form. She looked like a ghost.

I recognized her. She was the same woman I had seen in the water after my fall. I was sure of it. Spinning around, I raced toward the door. If I hurried, maybe I could catch her. It was evident she wanted to talk to me, or why else had she awoken me? I desperately wanted to speak with her. She was my link to finding the Star of Poison.

As I bounded across the floor, my foot slipped on a discarded T-shirt. Kieran's. I cursed him to hell and back while falling backward. With a loud thump, I landed on my ass, a shriek escaping my lips.

Kieran woke up with a start, his green eyes wide and aglow in the dark. They zeroed in on me sprawled over the floor. "What are you doing down there?"

I scrambled to my feet. "I need to do something. Hang on." I threw open the door.

"Olivia!" he bellowed, but I was already running down the hall.

Please let her still be there.

"Olivia!" Kieran yelled again, but this time he was chasing after me and gaining. If he caught me, I might never get my chance to talk to the ghost woman.

Whipping around the corner, I wound down the stairs, doing my best to be quick and not tumble all the way to the bottom. Kieran grabbed me around the waist before I could reach the first floor. "Let me go," I screeched, my feet struggling to touch the ground.

"What the hell is your deal?" he growled through his teeth, his python arms pinning me to him.

My body wriggled like a fish out of water, trying to break free. "I told you. There's something I need to do."

He took us down the last few steps to flat ground. "If you tell me what it is that has you jumping out of bed in the middle of the night, then we can discuss if it is a good idea."

I rolled my head back, letting it rest on Kieran's chest. "Gah! You're so frustrating."

"Thanks, Blondie."

We were wasting precious time. If I was going to have any chance of talking to her, I needed Kieran to trust me. "I saw someone outside," I confessed.

I couldn't see his face, but I knew he wore a look of consternation. "And you thought you would go check it out alone."

Silence.

He set me down on my feet and spun me around to face him, but wisely kept his hands on my shoulders in case I decided to bolt again. "Do I need to remind you there is a witch out there who would do everything in her power to kill you?"

"She needs me alive to find the stones," I pointed out stubbornly.

"Fine. But there are a million other things she could do to you."

We could argue all night, but then I would miss my opportunity. "I don't have time for this. Release me. Or come with me if you're afraid it's a trap."

Kieran studied me before exhaling, and I could see he was reluctant to let me free. "I better not regret this."

The moment his grasp loosened, I was running, but Kieran was quick, slipping his fingers into mine. I tugged him along with me, urging him to pick up the pace. My heart was in my throat when we burst outside, the evening wind blowing over my face. I froze as I glanced to the spot where I'd seen the woman.

There was no one. No ghost. No woman in a white dress. Disappointment dropped in my belly like a heavy stone, and my brain was in denial, but my instincts told me the woman had been here; I wasn't losing my marbles.

"Tianna is probably playing games with you." Kieran's deep voice came from beside me, his fingers squeezing mine in comfort.

I couldn't deny he might be right, but I didn't think so. The witch had been screwing with my mind and invading my dreams, and this felt different. "Maybe."

Swallowing hard, I moved farther into the courtyard, needing to make certain she had disappeared. The trees surrounding the castle danced with the wind, and I shivered.

I'm not going crazy. I'm not going to let her win.

Waking up, I felt like something Tianna had dug up from a witches' burial ground, something half alive. No rest for the wicked. It would take a month of sleep before I was human again; I didn't have a month, and I wasn't sure I'd ever be human again.

Any more nights like the one I'd had would damage my mental health.

Peeling my eyes open, I expected a stream of bright sunshine to greet me, or at the very least, Kieran's sexy grin. I got neither.

Alone in bed, I flipped over, peering out the window. The sky was gray and moody, mirroring my own feelings. Rain plummeted against the castle in a torrential down-pour. If it was raining outside that meant…

I jumped out of bed, thanking the storm gods. No

traipsing around in the woods! It felt like it was my birthday. All I needed was for Alice to bake me a cake. Ooo. Maybe I could get her to make me one. Chocolate for sure.

Stepping into the hall after throwing on some clothes, I scratched my head, looking left and then right. *Crap. Which way is the kitchen again?* I really needed to start asking for a map when I came to these castles. It would make getting around much easier.

Finding the stairs was simple enough, and I wound my way down to the first floor. I found Jase at the base on his way up. His hair was damp from a recent shower and combed away from his face. Blue cypress and seawater scented the air around him, making me want to breathe deeply.

"Hey, I was coming to check on you."

My fingers ran through my hair, while I tried to remember if I had brushed it before leaving my room. "No need. I saved you the trip."

His soft lips spread into a smile. "I heard about your late night adventure."

I guess it had been too much to hope that Kieran would have kept it to himself. The moss green tiles suddenly captured my attention. "It was a misunderstanding."

"Try again."

I lifted my gaze to his. His stubborn face told me he wasn't going to let this go. It crossed my mind to lie. Tianna would love that, and it could end up driving a wedge between Jase and me, which I definitely didn't want. "I see people."

"What does that mean?"

Unsure of how to explain it, I shrugged. "I haven't been able to figure out if I'm seeing things, or if they're ghosts, or if Tianna has cursed me, but I've seen two different women. The one in the lake at Wakeland was how I found the Star of Tranquility."

He shifted his weight to the other foot. "Why didn't you say anything?"

"I didn't want to sound like a crazy person." Of course, after everything I'd learned and seen, it didn't seem that crazy. Not in the Veil.

He shook his head at me. "A little too late for that."

"Are you going to insult me all day? Because if so, I have better things to do." I moved to brush past him, but Jase caught my hand, and tugged me to face him again.

"Not so quick, Cupcake. You and I have plans."

I groaned. "I'm not going to like this, am I?"

"Depends on your attitude, but it can be fun, if you let it." The impish gleam sparkling in his eyes made me wary.

"Does this mean I'm not getting a free day to just hang out?" Once the idea was rooted, I desperately wanted to spend hours doing absolutely nothing, recharging, and being lazy. Jase didn't share my sentiments.

"Funny. This is the perfect opportunity to practice controlling your tranquility skills."

"Exciting," I replied in a flat voice.

"That's the spirit," he added, clapping me on the back with overexaggerated enthusiasm.

Jase led me to the south end of Viperus Keep, to a room with whitewashed bricks, and a circular tiled floor. It was unlike any of the other rooms in the castle. Ivy hung down the walls as the storm pelted the glass ceiling overhead.

"Where are the others?" There should be someone else around in case things went south and I put Jase to sleep again.

He released my hand but stayed planted in front of the doorway, blocking my only exit. "They're searching the castle for anything that might help us find the Star of Poison."

I cleared my throat. "Shouldn't we be helping with that?"

Jase's low chuckle washed away my evasive response. "This is just as important. If we stand any chance of finding the stones, you need to learn how to deal with the power you received from the first stone."

Interlocking my hands behind my back, I wandered aimlessly around the room. "I've been meaning to ask, what happens when I find the next Star? Will I suddenly start poisoning everything?"

He forked a hand through his tousled hair. "I honestly don't know. We'll deal with it *if* it happens."

I swallowed; realizing I could do nothing about it now, so no point in stressing. My eyes shifted skyward, looking through the glass. Heavy rains continued to drench the transparent ceiling.

"Is this Tianna's doing?" I wasn't sure what made me ask, but something about the storm and her warning last night left me suspicious.

Jase's gaze followed mine to the glass dome above. "It smells like her witchcraft."

"I don't get it. Does she, or doesn't she want the Stars?"

"Don't ask me to understand the inner workings of a witch. I'm already fending off a dull pounding in my temples from this endless rain."

Fair enough. I squared my shoulders and planted my feet. "Okay, let's get this over with."

"Your excitement is contagious." He flashed me a twin set of those adorable little dimples.

His damn dimples were weapons that made my knees weak, but it was too late to create a defense against Jase's secret weapon. I didn't even bother to try, and let my heart cartwheel.

With my internal gymnastics unbeknownst to Jase, he got down to business. "I'm not going to pretend to know exactly how this will work, but I am betting your ability is like mine. The mechanics, whether I'm a dragon or a man, are the same."

"You huff, and you puff, and you knock them all down." I tried not to giggle.

"Something like that, but what you need to learn is how to turn it off and on. Inside you is the source of your power. It's like breathing two different types of air. One is the air you need to breathe, and the other is your weapon. Once you identify the difference between them in your lungs, you'll be able to choose which one to expel."

Unexpected anxiety dropped through me. "That sounds complicated."

The heat of his body swarmed over my skin as he moved to stand in front of me. He put his hands on my shoulders, applying light pressure to encourage me to sit on the floor. I complied. Jase sat across from me and took my hand in his. "Close your eyes," he instructed me.

"Why?" I countered.

He let out a low breath in exasperation at my obstinacy. "I want you to try something, and closing your eyes will help you get in touch with what is going on inside you."

I didn't like imagining magical things happening inside me that I couldn't see. Trusting Jase, I let my eyes drift shut. It wasn't like he would smash a pie in my face. "Now what?"

"First, you stop talking and questioning everything I say. Just listen. I'm guessing you've never meditated before."

Deliberately not speaking, I shook my head in response.

My eyes might be closed, but I could sense those lips of his curving. "Not a problem. I want you to concentrate on your breath as it goes in and out of your lungs, filling your chest and then leaving."

For a few minutes, I did just that, listening to the sound and feel of my breath. It was surprisingly relaxing.

The texture of his voice was smooth and put me at ease. "Do you notice anything unusual in your lungs?"

That didn't really make sense to me, but I nodded anyway, desperate to learn.

Jase's warm chuckle tickled my face. "You have no idea what I'm talking about."

I opened one eye and peeked at him, finding his closeness unnerving. A tingling thrill spiraled into my stomach. "Nope, but I really want to understand."

"You don't lack heart, that's for sure. Let's try again. Close your eyes, but this time when you're breathing, I want you to be conscious of how the air feels moving through your lungs. Tranquility has a different quality. Oxygen is clean and refreshing; it's natural. Tranquility is slightly cooler and smoother."

Trying again, I focused on the rise and fall of my chest. It took more effort this time to get back into the "me" zone. Jase's fingers, interwoven with mine, were distracting me to no end. If he wanted my full concentration, then he shouldn't have been softly stroking the pad of his thumb over my skin. But somehow I made it back to the land of Zen.

Time ticked by, and I was near the point of giving up when something funny happened in my chest. It was subtle, a light flutter of calmness. If I pointed all my attention to it, I could isolate it from the oxygen moving within me. The normal air didn't stop flowing, but with my focus solely on the tranquility inside me, I was filled with a peace I'd never felt before. It was all-encompassing, radiating from my chest to the tips of my toes to the crown of my head. The longer I concentrated on that cool breath in my lungs, the more it built until I had to let it go or explode.

My eyes slowly opened, and I blew out a gentle puff of air away from Jase's face. I don't know which of us was more excited. A wide smile spread over Jase's face as a cloud of lavender mist glided from my lips. I watched with a grin of my own as the sleeping vapors swirled and floated before evaporating. My eyes returned to his sparkling ones, and I resisted the urge to throw myself into his lap.

"That was amazing." I would be lying if I said I didn't

want to do it again.

Jase gave my knee a light squeeze. "See? All it takes is a bit of concentration."

Easy to say when it was second nature to you. "I can't believe I did it."

"Now to put it to the test, kiss me," he stated.

Jase didn't waste any time in his training methods. I'd managed to avoid not thinking about kissing any dragons for an hour, and here he was asking me to do just that. I blinked. "No."

He pursed his lips. "It isn't enough to identify the source of your power. You need to control it, and that comes with practice."

I tucked my hair behind my ears, nervous for so many reasons. Jase wanted me to kiss him. "And if I knock you out again?"

He tilted his head down to look me directly in the eyes. "Have a little faith, Cupcake. Isolate your tranquility and breathe."

How noble of him to willingly sacrifice himself. "Do you know who you're talking to? I can't believe you trust me. I don't even trust myself." Why was he taunting me? My mind was singularly focused on Jase's lips, and how addicting they were.

Dammit!

And he wasn't helping the situation. The pad of his thumb brushed against my lower lip, bringing my eyes to his. "You can do this."

I wet my lips. "Are you sure this isn't a ploy to get me to kiss you?"

He leaned in, bringing our lips closer. "What if it is?

Still doesn't change the fact that you need to learn how to switch it on and off."

I rolled my eyes. "Fine, but if you pass out, it's on you."

His finger hooked the top of my shirt. "Shut up and kiss me, Olivia."

He'd asked for it. Taking a deep breath, I tried to calm the sudden nerves that had snuck up on me. *It is just a kiss. No big deal, so stopping being so dramatic.* The little pep talk didn't help.

I leaned in, keeping my gaze zeroed in on his lips as I brought mine closer. My eyes fluttered closed, and then a surge of panic hit. I yanked back, my eyes flying open. "Wait! I'm not ready."

Jase's irises glowed. "You can't possibly be scared. Not the girl who jumped from a dragon's back to save me."

He had a point. When push came to shove, I could be brave.

Resting my wrists on his shoulders, I scooted closer. My mouth landed on his, and I completely forgot this was supposed to be a lesson. His lips were supple and gentle at first, but within seconds, he was claiming me, demanding more. I didn't need to be persuaded. The only thing that mattered was Jase's mouth, and how he made me feel like a flower in a patch of thorns. I lost myself in him, and any thought of tranquility ceased to exist. His tongue traced along my lips. I parted them for him.

The moment his tongue slipped against mine, a low moan escaped the back of my throat. My fingers dove into the silky strands of his hair. Somehow I ended up in his lap with my legs wrapped around him—neither of us eager to move away.

Warmth emanated from him, but it was more than his body heat. Our breaths mingled in a way that seemed as if they were connected, our abilities reaching out to each other. I didn't know how else to explain what was happening inside me.

"Fuck," Jase muttered, reluctantly, pulling away.

His fingers stayed framed against my face for a few pounding heartbeats. He pressed his forehead to mine. He had more restraint than I did, for I was ready to dive back in for seconds. He must have noticed the longing in my expression.

"I don't want you to lose your control," he explained, slipping a single arm around my waist. He lifted me to my feet.

"How was it?" I asked with an arrogant smile. I was feeling pretty smug about the kiss. He was still awake, which meant the kissing ban was over as long as I could control my tranquility.

"It was… good."

My hands fell to my sides. I was looking for "mind-numbing" or "boxer-dropping." "Good" did not stroke my ego. "Gee, thanks. You know how to make a girl feel special."

A serious frown spread over his face, marring his handsome features. "I'm doing my best to keep my hands off you, and not strip you out of that dress. Is that *good* enough for you?"

I gulped, secretly pleased.

Holy crap. I had power. Like actual inhuman ability. I was a goddamn superhero.

The wind flew over my face as I squeezed my knees together, holding onto Kieran's back for dear life. Riding a dragon was the most exhilarating experience in the world. It wasn't possible, but I wished everyone could try it at least once in their life. I took advantage whenever a descendant was willing to take me. Today, though, had been a case of Kieran demanding I come rather than me begging.

A few days had passed since my lesson with Jase. Zade had stayed with me last night, and apparently Kieran couldn't wait because he had come bursting in to wake us up. Still half asleep, I had sat up in bed and rubbed my eyes, only to have a pile of random clothes tossed at me.

"Get dressed, Blondie. We're going for a ride."

Zade had rolled over and groaned, giving Kieran the middle finger.

I couldn't get dressed fast enough.

Rolling out of the extra toasty bed, I threw on the clothes, and rushed to follow Kieran downstairs and out the front door. He was already in his dragon form by the time I caught up to him, waiting for me to climb onto his back. His triangle head angled over his shoulder, to keep an eye on me as I positioned myself, and held on tightly.

Dark, ominous clouds painted the sky around us in shades of gray and green. Below us, various shapes of green leaves blanketed the tops of the trees. Kieran kept us above the woods to make our route more direct, but we flew close enough to them to take shelter if needed. So far, the coast had been clear.

No wraiths. No griffins. No witches. I enjoyed the peace for once.

"It feels wonderful to be outside."

His eyes trained on the cliffs in the distance. *"The storm isn't gone yet. It will rain again. And soon."*

The reminder of our gloomy weather turned my thoughts to Tianna. I didn't delude myself into thinking this was a joy ride. Everything the descendants did was for a purpose. "Where are we going?"

"There is a place that might be able to help." His voice sounded in my head. When the descendants were in dragon form, they could communicate through projecting thoughts. It was pretty kick-ass.

My fingers glided over Kieran's emerald scales as I lowered myself closer to his thick neck. "Why aren't the others with us?"

"They needed to check on their kingdoms. Make sure Tianna hasn't done anything insane in their absence."

Made complete sense to me, but I still missed them. It was always so quiet when we weren't all together. "So what provoked this impromptu trip?"

"Ever since you told us about the apparitions you've been seeing, it got me thinking. I don't believe they're a coincidence. The others agree, and there is one place in the Veil that might give us answers about what they mean."

Kieran thinking… this should be interesting. At least they didn't think I was crazy.

"It is a place deep in Viperus. Hopefully, something sparks."

He was being awful cryptic, which made me uneasy, but flying on a dragon had a way of making it less worrisome. We flew for maybe another ten or fifteen minutes— my concept of time had been skewed since living in the Veil. They didn't bind their lives to the clock.

Kieran landed on his hind legs first before his front claws touched the ground. Jostled from the movement, I tightened my legs, and the bag strapped to my back slipped off one shoulder. I steadied myself, before trying to slip down the side of him. Kieran crouched flat, and I made my move, swinging both legs to the side so I could jump off him.

Safely on two feet, I wiggled the bag off my shoulders and waited for Kieran to shift. I couldn't help but watch. It was marvelous to witness the beast morphing into a man. How their bodies were capable of such drastic transformations boggled my mind. I didn't know if I would ever be able to wrap my head around it.

Or their lack of modesty. Being naked never seemed to faze them, unless I was naked. That was an entirely different ball game.

I handed over the bag, and Kieran pulled out the clothes he'd brought along. As he got dressed, I busied myself by taking in our surroundings. Kieran had dropped us outside a cave made entirely of trees. Thick, lush leaves formed the entrance. Compelled by a mysterious force, I walked through the arch of tree branches and into the mouth of the cave. At the center of the chamber was a pool with sparkling turquoise water. Humid air rose in a mist from the water's surface like a sauna.

"What is this place?" I asked, as my eyes absorbed the snippet of paradise.

And then a snake slithered across the grassy floor, right past my toes.

All hell broke loose.

I screamed, as I was prone to do at the sight of slimy critters with forked tongues. The shriek issuing from my throat was long and could have woken the dead.

Kieran was quick to react. Shirtless, he bolted in front of me, sealing my mouth shut with his hand. "Shh. It won't hurt you."

I begged to differ. Just its presence in the same room as me hurt.

With owl-sized eyes, I whacked Kieran on the chest. "Why didn't you tell me we were entering a snake's den," I hissed from behind his hand, which still covered my mouth.

"It's not a snake's den. It's the Mirrored Shallows." He removed his hand from my mouth, smiling the entire time.

My gaze shifted left and then right. "Is it gone?"

"Yes, the big, meanie reptile has left."

No longer feeling threatened or afraid of having a snake inject its venom into my calf, I strolled along the uneven ground. "What's so special about this place?" I couldn't deny its splendor, but I didn't see how it would help our current situation, and yet, if the descendants had brought me here, there must be a good reason.

"The Mirrored Shallows is said to be the thinnest point of the Veil. It is here where the living can see the dead, and…" He let his voice trail off.

"And what?" I prompted. He couldn't leave me dangling with something like that.

"And where the dead can summon the living," his deep voice finished.

I swallowed. Things were starting to come together. "You want to see if I can talk to the woman who keeps appearing to me since I stepped foot in Viperus," I concluded.

He nodded. "That is the plan. You game?"

My eyes jumped to the pool, studying it intently before darting back to Kieran. "Why not? It isn't the weirdest thing I've done since coming to the Veil." I walked up to the edge of the water with cautious steps and glanced down. "What do I do?"

Kieran's shadow fell over me, the spikes from his hair reflecting in the water. "You get in."

Nothing in the Veil was ever as simple as it seemed. There was always a catch, and I guessed the little hiccup would reveal itself in due time. "Have you ever gone in?"

He nodded. "Many times… especially after the war. I thought if I could see my father, he might be able to help us defeat Tianna, and break her curse."

I didn't have to ask the outcome of those visits, especially, when a touch of sadness moved into his eyes. "No chance you brought me a change of clothes in that bag, is there?" I quickly changed the topic.

"I figured you'd air dry on the way back."

Good thing I wore one of those flimsy dresses that were so popular in the isles. Kicking off my slip-on shoes, I hiked up the hem of my dress and dipped my toes in to test the water. The temperature was pleasant. Not as balmy as the bathhouse at Wakeland castle, or the water-fall shower at Viperus Keep, but it wasn't a deal breaker. Pushing forward, I went deeper into the pool, and a chill rushed over my legs. The eeriness increased until my skin was coated with it. I paused at the center, turning around to face Kieran. Water lapped around me while I treaded, but it quickly stilled. Almost too quickly.

"Now what?" I inquired, kicking my feet lightly to keep me afloat.

Kieran sat at the edge of the water—close enough to reach me if something happened—but he made sure to not let the water touch him. "You take a deep breath and go under, Blondie."

Letting my hands skim the surface, I stared down into the water. Even though it wasn't deep, I couldn't see the bottom of the pond. The color beneath me grew darker until it was nearly black. Inhaling a breath of air, I braced myself and dunked my head under the surface.

The first thing I noticed was the cold as the water touched my face, but then came the voices. It sounded like I was at a concert, everyone talking and screaming at once over the music. I wanted to plug my ears and push to the surface, but I forced myself to stay under the water, relaxing my limbs. My heart galloped in my chest.

One at a time, I yelled in my head.

No one was more surprised than me when the voices ceased for a blissful few seconds. *Finally, souls that listen to me.*

A soft female voice laughed in the water, the sound surrounding me from all sides. My head turned left and right, looking for the source of the feminine voice. A bright ball of light moved toward me, and I realized the voice came from the light. Her blurry form slowly began to take shape in the murky waters below me. Beautiful waves of blonde hair swirled around her face. Wisps of her white dress tangled with her feet. She was the woman I'd seen before.

"Olivia." She spoke my name. *"You should not have come here. The witch is searching for you."*

I didn't bother to ask how she knew who I was. *"I had no choice. We must find the Star of Poison."*

Alarm captured her eyes. *"It is not safe here. She isn't the only one who would do you harm."*

"The other souls?" I guessed, thinking about the mass of voices in the water when I had gone under.

Her round head nodded. *"They are restless, eager to be released from this world."*

"What do they think I'm trying to do?" I shot back in aggravation.

Her pinkish-blue lips curled. *"The dead aren't reasonable."*

Kind of like the descendants.

Her slim hand extended, caressing the side of my cheek. *"They don't care how the barrier is broken, only that it is. You will face many obstacles in your quest to release the dragons from their curse."*

My body floated with little effort on my part, neither rising nor sinking, just suspended in the dark waters. *"Is there no way you can help me? I can't fail."*

Despair radiated from her, and it stabbed me in the heart. *"No, you can't. We're all depending on you."*

No pressure. *"I don't know what to do or where to look."*

Soft aqua light haloed her body. *"The Stars are drawn to the hearts of the dragon descendants. They will return to a place of importance and meaning to those who rule the land."*

Her idea of help wasn't very concrete. *"Who are you?"* I asked, still uncertain if she was someone trustworthy.

"My name is—"

I was yanked from the water by a pair of strong arms.

"Son of a bitch," I swore, shoving strands of dripping hair out of my face. I stared into Kieran's glowing emerald eyes. His arms were secured around me, keeping me pinned to his chest. "Couldn't you have waited a few more seconds before fishing me out of the water?"

"I thought you were dead," he growled, frowning at me. It took me aback. Kieran never scowled or scolded me. "You were underwater for far too long. And when I called your name, you didn't respond."

Really? It had felt like seconds to me. "I was fine... I think. I was doing what you wanted, trying to get information."

We were both soaking wet, our clothes plastered against our skin. Beads of water rolled down his chest. "You saw something?"

I bit my lip and nodded. "The same woman as before when I fell into the hole."

"What did she say? Did she tell you where to find the Star of Poison?"

Squeezing the water out of my hair, I looked at him sideways. "I was working on it, but you pulled me out before I could get more details. She said that the Stars are drawn to each of you, and would return to a place of meaning."

Kieran scrunched his face. "Is that all she said?"

"Do you want me to go back under?"

We both glanced over at the mystical pool of souls. "Definitely not. It's not safe."

"That's what she said." A shiver rolled through me.

Kieran's hands moved up and down my arms, bringing warmth to my skin. "It's time for us to go, Blondie."

I nodded, eager to get out of this little tree cave. The Mirrored Shallows wasn't a place I'd hang out at, or linger. As we crossed through the branched archway, a bolt of angry lightning cracked in the sky, coming awfully close to the tops of the trees that canopied us. Kieran's arms went around me, tightening. "The storm is back."

My body tensed. "I guess flying is out of the question."

Kieran gave the sky a dark glare. "It is for the moment. We'll wait out the storm until Tianna gets bored of torturing us."

Like that was ever going to happen. "It is going to be a long day," I said, stepping out of Kieran's embrace, and walking around the entrance to the tree cave that would be our shelter from the storm. A chill entered the air. If it kept up, I would freeze to death. My teeth started to chatter. Too bad Zade wasn't nearby; I could use a dose of his flames.

Kieran came to my rescue with a T-shirt in his hand. "We need to get you dried off. Here, put this on, and I'll see if I can start a fire."

As he gathered branches from the ground, I slipped out of my wet clothes and put on the soft shirt. It smelled of Kieran—exotic and wild. Dipping my head, I brought up the collar of the shirt to my nose, and inhaled, nuzzling the material against my face. How could any human smell so incredibly good? But the thing was, I felt exactly the same about the others. They each had their own unique scent that tempted me.

Within minutes, Kieran had a little fire going inside of the tree cave. Probably not the safest place, considering all the wood, but the alternative was no shelter. I stood beside the flickering flames with my hands out, letting its heat seep into my body.

"How are we going to let the others know we're okay?" I asked, concerned they might try to track us down in this magically induced shit-storm. It wasn't like the Veil had cell phone service.

"They'll know we sought cover. It's what any of us would do." Kieran seemed confident about the matter. I decided if he wasn't going to worry, then neither would I. "You should rest."

Spending the night in a cave filled with the souls of the dead creeped me the fuck out, I didn't know if I could do it. Sleep would not come easily. "Not happening. How do I know one of those souls swimming around in that pool won't try to possess my body in my sleep?"

"I doubt that would happen."

"Really? So far, everything I've seen of the Veil suggests otherwise."

Kieran gave the dark pool a distressed stare. "You might be right."

I rolled my eyes. That was likely the first time I'd ever heard one of them admit I was right about something. I wanted to treasure the moment, but the gleam that had suddenly sprung into Kieran's eyes had my blood racing.

"We'll have to do something else to occupy our time."

My head tilted to the side. "And what do you have in mind?"

He flashed me a grin, and hope fluttered in my belly. "I'm thinking you need more than a fire to warm you up."

"Ha," I breathed.

He still stood directly across from me on the other side of the fire, but he could feel the tension in the air between us, and the twitch of his lips told me he was going to do something devious. Wickedly devious I hoped.

"Is that a challenge?"

I shifted under his roguish gaze, wondering what he would do or say next, because I was a tangle of excited nerves. My eyes flicked to the fire, searching for something clever to say in response. I had nothing.

"Olivia," Kieran murmured my name, his voice suddenly so much closer.

I spun toward the sound, not expecting him to be at my side. How the hell had he moved so fast? My hands steadied themselves on his shoulders before I fell into the fire. Just what I needed: to go up in flames.

Blinking, I registered the warm skin under my fingers.

He is shirtless, my brain reminded me. Why yes, he was. My eyes became distracted by his bronze chest. I'd seen all of the descendants naked, but it never grew tiresome. With hesitant fingers, I traced the tattoo lines on Kieran's chest. The black ink covered his entire right pectoral, trailing down to his flat belly and over his hip. The design spidered over his body, like the roots of a tree.

Air hissed through his teeth when my fingers skirted the band of his jeans. His hand shot out, capturing my wrist. My eyes snapped up, and the emotion stirring in his face caused my heart to pound. With a quick jerk, my breasts laid against his chest and my hips snuggled into his. Dear God. The feel of him pressed to the soft parts of me sent my pulse racing.

Wow. He was really hard.

And I wasn't just talking about his abs.

What am I doing?!

Flirting with danger.

His fingers framed my face, and I was hypnotized by the luminosity of his eyes. "I'm going to kiss you now." His husky voice melted my insides.

How could I say no to a kiss? "I might knock you out with my breath."

Bending his head, his lips curled. "I'll take my chances."

His soft lips closed over mine, and I felt like he'd drugged me. The storm raging outside, and the souls swimming in the bottom of the eerie pool were whisked from my mind. Every wonderful sensation brought on by the taste of his lips magnified in other parts of my body. His mouth slanted across mine, his tongue slipping past my inexperience. The velvety softness of his lips, combined with the rasp of his tongue, drew a purr from my core.

A blush stole over my body.

Kieran diverted his lips off to the side near my cheek. "I don't just want to kiss you, Olivia," he murmured in my ear, before taking my lobe in between his teeth. I pressed my lips together to keep from moaning. "Do you understand what I'm asking?"

Wait. What was he saying? If only he would stop doing that thing with his tongue. It was making it beyond difficult to concentrate, but when his words finally registered, a tornado of need swept through me. *Oh, my god. He wanted to sleep with me? Don't freak out. Do I want to sleep with Kieran?*

Yes! Yes! Hell yes!

But I needed to make one thing very clear. Waves of tension mounted inside me, as Kieran continued to rain succulent kisses down my throat, and over my neck. My fingers pressed at his chest, and I could feel myself slowly going under again.

No, not yet. You have something to tell him.

I applied pressure. "Wait." His mouth was reluctant to leave the alcove of my neck, but he peered down at me with heavily lidded eyes. "You need to know something before this goes any further."

"I want to make you mine," he growled, his eyes glowing brightly. "And I can feel how much you desire me."

Damn emotional bond.

His head dipped to take possession of my lips. He wasn't going to make this easy. My body was already leaning back toward him, but I pulled myself together.

"Kieran, if you kiss me again, I won't get this out, and it's important."

He had to know that I had feelings for the others. He would have sensed it, so what I was about to say shouldn't be a surprise.

I hoped.

Taking a shaky breath, I prepared to say what was on my mind. "I need you to know that whatever happens between us, it doesn't change my feelings for the others."

His lips skimmed my jaw. "I know."

It took me a moment to respond. "And you're okay with that?"

He gave a one-shoulder shrug. "For the first time in a hundred years, we have hope, and it is because of you. I don't know how this will work with the four of us, but I do know I need you in my life." Kieran stroked the pad of his thumb over my bottom lip, and I shuddered.

Good enough for me. I'd figure the *other* stuff out later.

Before I even finished nodding, he was kissing me. Leaning into his lips, my mind sighed. *Finally*. But my body was not appeased. It wanted so much more. And Kieran was happy to oblige. His hands slipped to my hips, gathering the hem of my T-shirt and pushing it up past my waist. Those fingers skimmed over my skin, leaving behind electric tingles.

I was going to come undone before we even got to the good stuff.

As his mouth claimed mine, I reveled in wonderment, I was about to have sex with a dragon in a tree cave.

Who would believe me?

None of that mattered.

I no longer gave two shits about what other people thought of me. Maybe my new attitude was also why I was so willing to accept my situation—me and four dragon shifters. It was complicated, sure, but being with Kieran like this made it seem worth it.

He secured an arm around my lower back and lifted me up. My legs automatically wrapped like a pretzel around his waist. It felt like I was flying. No, not flying. Kieran was laying us down, his body cushioning mine from the rock and dirt floor. I continued my exploration of his glorious body, running my fingers over the thick muscles of his arms. His golden skin was magnificent.

Kieran was a sweet intoxication and I couldn't get enough. My fingers fumbled with the button on his pants, brushing over a faint dusting of dark hair that led straight into his jeans. I wanted to be rid of all barriers. Kieran must have felt the same way. Within seconds, my shirt was up and over my head, discarded to some corner of the hollow. His pants followed, and just like that, we were skin to skin.

"I've never seen anyone as beautiful as you," he whispered.

Coming from any other guy, I would have blown off his admiration, but Kieran had never sounded more sincere or serious in his life, so much so that even I believed I was beautiful. I didn't know what to say. Thank you seemed too commonplace, so I laced my fingers in his hair and brought my lips down to his. The kiss seemed to last forever, a kiss filled with dreams, magic, desire.

Things escalated quickly.

I couldn't keep track of his hands as they roamed over my body, from my shoulders to my belly, to my thighs, and all the places in between. His lips spread fire everywhere they touched me, and passion burned between us. When his hot mouth closed over my breast, my spine arched forward as I reeled with pleasure.

What is he doing to me?

My hips moved, rubbing over the hardness of him with brisk, stimulating gyrations. I didn't know what I was doing, but I couldn't control myself. The amazing feelings were building and building. The primal need for release was overwhelming my sanity. And still, it frightened me. I'd never felt this kind of powerful emotion coursing through me.

But something I did recognize rose up inside me. Tranquility.

Breaking off the kiss, I turned my head to the side, to keep my breath away from Kieran's face. If he passed out on me right before the end, I would be pissed. He didn't seem to notice the sudden shift in my demeanor, but it didn't matter because he aligned our bodies. And slowly I was filled with heat, deeply, and completely filled. Kieran was enchanting, his hands, his lips, his body—the whole package. There was no going back.

His teeth scraped over my collarbone, and I arched against him, our bodies moving together in perfect harmony. I never wanted this night to end. My nails scored his back, and tendrils of wild desire rushed to the surface. Together we reached the edge, and tumbled over it blissfully. The orgasm rocked my entire body.

Glowing from the inside out, I purred in contentment, twisting into his arms. He pressed a soft kiss to my glistening neck and then to my cheek. A storm brewed outside, and I was curled cozily against Kieran, happier than I'd been in a long time.

Holy shit. I'd just slept with a dragon.

None of the girls at my old high school could say that. And Jimmy Whitt had nothing on Kieran. Jimmy had been my first, and last experience with sex. I'd never wanted to repeat that painful deed again, until I met the descendants. It amazed me how vastly different the experience had been with someone who knew what he was doing. Now I wanted to experience all of them. Jase. Zade. And Issik.

Would it be different each time?

That thought generated another, not so pleasant, one. What would I tell the others? Should I say anything? I rested my chin on Kieran's chest, watching his face highlighted by the amber flames.

"Don't tell the others. Not yet. The last thing I need is you guys fighting over me… more than usual," I added.

He grinned. "That's not likely to happen. We're dragons. Fighting is what we do."

"Don't I know it," I muttered. "But jealousy won't help us find the stones."

His fingers brushed a lock of golden hair off my face. "If that is what you wish."

"It is." We lay quietly together, still absorbed in the afterglow of what we'd done. "Can I ask you a question?"

"Always, Blondie."

"How do you keep control of your poison in a… situation like this?"

Kieran raised an arm behind his head as a cushion. "You mean while making love?"

My fingers played with the fine hairs that ran down his lower stomach. "I guess."

"Were you afraid I would poison you?"

I shook my head. "I was afraid I would tranq you."

He considered my worried face. "It takes time. I've had over a hundred years to learn to harness my dragon gift. There will be times you'll forget or lose control, but at least tranquility won't kill anyone." I picked up on traces of remorse in his voice.

Had people died while Kieran had learned to master his poison?

I didn't ask, for the memories seemed painful, and I didn't want to tarnish what we had shared by drudging up the past.

The room had gone silent other than the crackling of the dwindling fire in front of us. "It sounds like the storm might be letting up," Kieran added. "We should get back to the castle before Tianna decides to flood Viperus in her bad mood."

If this was Tianna sulking, I didn't want to see what happened when we found another Star, because I was determined to show this witch up. Untangling ourselves, we gathered our clothes, and I got dressed by the glowing firelight while Kieran stuffed his in the bag. I wasn't sure if things were different between Kieran and me, or if it was my imagination. Should I say something? Thank you?

Definitely not.

Neither of us spoke, but it wasn't awkward like I remembered those moments following my first time with eight-seconds Jimmy being. I peeked up at Kieran, seeing him move toward the arched entrance. It was dark, but I could make out the form of his naked shadow as he stepped outside the Mirrored Shallows. He was preparing to shift, and it was a sight I didn't want to miss.

Rushing to catch up with Kieran, I grabbed the bag off the floor and secured it onto my back. The cool midnight air jolted my senses, and I huddled deeper into Kieran's T-shirt, letting the scent of him envelop me as I climbed onto my waiting chariot.

His wings beat, whipping the wind as we climbed

through the air. Unfortunately, our flight home was not destined to be unadventurous.

We'd barely left the Mirrored Shallows, when a trio of griffins flew in from behind the gloomy clouds, flanking Kieran on both sides with one hovering directly over my head. I fucking hated these lion-birds. They were really making my life a living hell, and they had to ruin what had turned out to be a pretty mind-blowing night.

"Kieran!" I called.

"Hang on. Things are going to get a little rough."

Wonderful.

Kieran dodged left and then right, doing his best to evade the griffins as they attempted to claw or snap at him. It was too long before I figured out their plan, tricky little assholes. The two alongside kept Kieran distracted while the one above me was waiting for his moment. It came before I had a chance to warn Kieran.

The griffin dove for me, his claws extended.

"Olivia, duck!" Kieran ordered me in a deep growl.

Quickly, I did as he instructed, flattening myself against his back, as the griffin above my head swooped down. His nails drug along my back, shredding Kieran's shirt and slicing my skin. I cried out but held on tight, breathing through the pain. Shit. That would leave a nasty mark, but their plan had failed… this time.

"That was close. Are you hurt?" Kieran asked, weaving through the air.

"I'm fine," I lied through my teeth, curling my fingers against him to keep the agony from my voice.

"I've got to get you out of here. We're going for the trees where we can hopefully lose them. I want you to run as soon as

we touch the ground. Do you understand? They want to take you prisoner. I can't let that happen."

"I got it." My heart was jackhammering in my chest.

"Whatever happens, don't let go of me."

I didn't think I could hold on any tighter, but Kieran tested my strength. Diving toward the earth, he flipped around, exposing his underbelly to the griffins as we fell backward. He opened his mouth, releasing a mist of green poison.

Take that, you feathery abominations.

The trio of griffins squawked, scrambling to avoid the mist, but they had been following us too closely. Kieran's poison worked its way into their lungs, sealing their fate. I bet that would piss off a certain witch. The griffins' eyes bulged as if they were suffocating. Their feathered wings flapped haphazardly in the air before they completely stopped moving at all. Then they fell—nothing but dead weight.

We exhaled simultaneously. Using the force of his wings, Kieran spun us around, regaining control of our flight. *"Are you—?"*

Out of nowhere, a crack of thunder boomed like a god roaring from the heavens. It was followed by a spear of lightning so bright that I was blinded for a few seconds. In that short time, I didn't realize the bolt of light had struck my dragon.

Tumbling, spinning, spiraling downward in a breathless rush toward the ground, we fell from the sky. My fingers clutched Kieran as I hung on for dear life. The world became a dizzy blur of dark colors and fear.

Holy shit. We're going to die.

11

"I won't let you die."

I swore I heard Kieran's voice in my head, but his wings remained unmoving, and at any moment, we were going to smack into the ground.

Oh, my god. What am I going to do?

If there was a plan worth hatching, my brain was in too much shock to think of it. I did the only thing I could. Scream.

I don't know how he managed it, but right before we hit the forest below, Kieran spun. I was jostled off his back, free-falling. But not for long. His claws scooped me out of the air, brought me to his chest, nestling me against him. Panic tore through my gut.

Branches and leaves lashed his large form from all sides, snapping under his speed and weight. Our death was imminent. And all I could think was, at least I'd been loved fully and completely.

We hit the ground with an impact that shook the world. It rumbled like an earthquake, and the force of

Kieran's fall seemed to crack the ground. The oxygen in my lungs vanished, leaving me gasping for breath.

And then nothing.

For a moment, I feared I'd died and all this fuzzy green shit I saw was Hell, but then my vision cleared. With the help of the moon, I collected pieces of my location, slowly remembering all the events that had led to this point.

I should be dead.

But by a miracle, I wasn't. In fact, I was very much alive and well. Sprawled over Kieran's underbelly, I pushed myself upright. Kieran had landed directly on his back in an attempt to keep me cradled, and safe from the brunt of the fall.

Stupid dragon!

He put himself in jeopardy to save me. I would never forgive him if he didn't wake up. If he…

I couldn't bring myself to finish the thought.

Scrambling up his long torso toward his neck, I used the scales on his body as handholds to prevent me from tumbling off him. He wasn't moving, and from what I could tell, he wasn't breathing either.

Don't do this to me. Don't leave me out here alone. You can't leave me. I forbid it!

I reached his neck, frantically searching for a pulse. Relief and wonder poured through me as I felt his heart beating strong against my ear.

Kieran was alive, but that didn't mean he was out of danger.

I needed to get help because—let's be real—how the hell was I going to save him? This wasn't the type of wound I could slap a Band-Aid on, kiss it better, and call it a day. He was unconscious, and bleeding in more places than I could keep pressure on at once. Not to mention dragging a dragon through the woods was an impossible task, almost like finding a stone. No way. I had to find help.

Flipping around on my ass, I slid down Kieran's side, landing on a pair of wobbly legs. I laid a hand on his dragon cheek, feeling the textured scales on my palm. "Don't move. Don't stop breathing. Don't die. I'm going to get you help and save you," I vowed.

Now was the time to be a hero. I wished I had wings. It would have made getting to Viperus Keep that much quicker, for time was Kieran's enemy. Without wasting another second, I took off, racing through the woods. The castle wasn't far—less than a mile or two. I never would have found my way if it weren't for the moonlight catching the eyes of the snake that wound up Viperus Keep. They glinted like a pair of twin lighthouses leading me home.

My legs were weak as I ran through the thicket of trees, keeping the top of the castle in view. I stumbled over rocks, twigs, and my own two feet more times than I could count, but I never stopped. The sounds of the woods echoed around me—crickets, animals howling, and the husky sound of a woman laughing.

Wait.

That wasn't normal.

I faltered.

Tianna.

Was she out there? Waiting for me? Or was she enjoying the torment she'd created with her spells and demented mind?

Truthfully, right now I didn't give a witch's tit.

Fueled by the desire to not let Tianna win, I continued running, and didn't stop until I burst through the front door of Viperus Keep. It was then I remembered what Kieran had said about the other descendants going to check on their lands.

"Hello!" I yelled, my voice carrying up to the high ceilings.

Please let them be back here. I didn't know what I would do if not a single descendant was here.

"Olivia, you're home," Alice said, stepping into the room. She wore a white apron around her waist.

"Are the others here?" I asked, breathless and anxious. "It's Kieran. He's hurt. Bad."

Alice's hand flew over her mouth, concern brightening her eyes. "Oh my. Yes. They are pacing the great room worrying about you."

Before I had a chance to head in the direction of the great room, Jase, Zade, and Issik stormed into the hall and pounced on me.

"Where the hell have you been?" Jase hissed. His dark hair was ruffled like he'd been raking his fingers through it, as he was known to do when stressed.

"Do you know how worried we've been?" Zade added, fire burning in his whiskey-colored eyes.

Issik gave me a frosty once-over, taking in my scuffed and battered state. "I'm going to kill Kieran."

My head shook back and forth, beseeching them with my eyes. "You might not get the chance. Hurry. You must help him."

Jase's brows drew together. "What are you talking about? What happened?"

Lurching forward, I grabbed his hand, tugging it with all my might. "I don't have time to explain. He's hurt. Tianna. We must go now before it's too late!"

Somehow through my broken, panicked phrases, they put together the pieces. Without another word, Issik burst into his dragon and took off through the front door to the sky. Zade followed with scales of crimson and gold papering his flesh.

I was no longer pulling Jase. He was dragging me through the doors of Viperus Keep. "You're going to tell me everything that happened as we fly."

I nodded. Fear choked my throat.

Jase tossed back his head, letting the dragon take over. He stood before me, his muscular form filling the court-yard, and his angular head standing tall and proud. Bright violet eyes stared down at me. With a nudge of his head, he pushed me up onto his back. *"Where's Kieran?"*

"In the woods not far from here. There." I pointed off to the north where I'd emerged from moments ago. "He fell from the sky. The griffins attacked, and as soon as Kieran had taken care of them, Tianna struck him down."

"We'll find him," Jase vowed. He had never broken a promise to me. *"If he was seriously injured, his body would have changed back by now to heal."*

"That's a thing?" I asked, my voice shaking. I hadn't realized I was trembling.

"Yes, Cupcake. I'm told we're not easy to kill, not even by a witch, much to her displeasure."

"I was so scared."

"You're safe now. We never should have let you go." A tingle of power radiated over my skin. Tranquility, the ability I shared with this particular dragon. It connected us.

Jase landed in the clearing created by Kieran's fall. Issik and Zade were right beside us. Jase had been right. Kieran was in his human form, naked, and curled up on the ground. I bounded off Jase, rushing to Kieran's side, needing to make sure he was still breathing—that we weren't too late. Jase might be confident Kieran would recover—that his body would heal itself—but I needed to see it with my own eyes. Some magic needed to be seen.

I dropped down to my knees, running my fingers over his chest. He was shivering. "Blondie," he croaked, his voice rough and raspy.

My eyes flashed to his. Their usual bright sparkle was dull. I wrapped my hand around his. "I'm here. I brought the others as I promised."

His fingers gave a light squeeze against mine, but it was weak. "You shouldn't have put yourself in danger. I-I'll be fine."

Just like a dragon to think nothing could hurt him.

"You were struck by lightning and fell out of the sky," I not so eloquently reminded him. "I don't care who you are. You could have died."

His lips curled. "But I didn't."

Jase shifted while Zade and Issik both stayed in their dragon forms. "We need to get him back to the castle. He'll recover quicker in his home."

113

I wiped at my cheeks, surprised to find them wet. I was crying, finally letting the events of the day catch up to me. All I wanted to do was turn around and launch myself into Jase's arms, bury my face into his chest, and sob like a baby, but I couldn't. Not yet.

Kieran still needed me.

Stiffening my chin, I nodded. Together, Jase and I were able to get Kieran to his feet. His large frame leaned heavily on Jase for support. Issik flattened to the ground, allowing us to hoist Kieran onto his back.

Jase touched my shoulder, bringing my attention to him. He searched my face, and I could see he wanted to offer me comfort as much as I wanted him. Giving in, he wrapped me in his arms. "Zade will take you back to the castle. I'll make sure this fool doesn't fall off."

The crimson dragon was waiting for me. Jase released me and lifted me up onto Zade before hopping onto Issik's back behind Kieran, who was draped over the side. In a crisis, the descendants seemed to be able to coordinate together seamlessly without having to say a thing. It was odd and impressive, but at the moment, I didn't care how they did it, only that Kieran was safe.

I hugged my arms around Zade, resting my cheek on his neck. Fatigue crashed over me. My body ached, too worn to hold itself up. Zade was there for me—my strength, my wings, my protector. He kicked off, taking us swiftly back to the castle. The warmth of his body seeped into mine, and I reveled in the heat. I was so cold.

"We're almost home," he promised.

My cheek pressed against his scales. They were smoother than they appeared. "He's going to be okay, isn't he?" I knew what Jase had said, and I'd heard Kieran pretend like this was no big deal, but I couldn't shake the feeling that what had happened was monumental.

"Of course," Zade assured me, but his voice didn't hold the amount of confidence I sought.

"Do you actually believe that, or are you saying that so I don't worry?"

I was met with silence.

That's what I thought. My heart was battering against my chest, and what was a five-minute flight seemed like hours. I felt as if Zade was lagging behind on purpose, to give Issik and Jase time to tend to Kieran. But they kept insisting he would be fine. It was hard to believe. I wanted to trust that Kieran would be his healthy, smirking, flirty self in no time, but my nagging intuition told me something else was at play here, and the descendants didn't want me to find out what it was.

That was laughable.

If I could find the Star of Tranquility, a stone that had been missing for decades, surely I could uncover whatever secret they were hiding.

By the time I got back to the castle, and wrestled my way past the dragon muscle wall, Kieran was in his bed recovering. I crossed the room slowly, unable to take my eyes off his face. Most of the surface cuts and scratches had already healed. The only remnant of his trauma was the dried blood in his hair. Tears welled in my eyes, and my lower lip trembled. The adrenaline had begun to wear off, leaving me stunned at how close we'd come to dying.

"Those wouldn't be tears I see in your eyes, would they?" Kieran rasped.

Swallowing, I dabbed at my cheeks. "I think I deserve a sob fest."

The sparkle in his expression sobered, darkening his emerald eyes. "I put you in danger. I won't ever forgive myself."

Tears blurred my vision; I couldn't hold them at bay anymore. "That's bullshit. If you think I would have survived that without you—survived any of this—then you're crazy."

As I hoped, a small smirk emerged on his face. "That might be true, but I can attest that I'm somewhat crazy."

With care, I sat on the edge of the bed and gave a short laugh. "The four of you really are. Are you going to be okay?"

He shifted on the bed to sit up, but frustration overcame his expression at the difficulty of the everyday movement. Switching tactics, he stayed lying down, and reached for my hand instead. "Nothing a few hours of rest won't cure."

"How did I know you were going to say that?" He was nuts. I planned to sleep for a week, if only I could. Tianna made it impossible. I had a stone to find and couldn't afford to take off any time. Kieran might not die today or tomorrow, but unless I found that stone soon—very soon —he could still die. They all could.

And I would never be able to live with myself... live without them.

These four dragons had become not only the most important people in my life, but also the only people in my life. I needed them as much as they needed me, probably more so, and I refused to let Tianna take them from me.

Leaning over Kieran, I brushed my lips across his. "Get some sleep."

I needed to get to work ASAP.

As I got up to leave, Kieran grabbed my wrist, and I stared back at him. "I know that look. Don't do anything stupid," he warned me.

Best not to make a promise I couldn't keep. "The last thing you need to do is worry about me. There are three other dragons to do that."

His fingers gently fell away from my wrist, and I stepped out into the hallway. As soon as I was out of Kieran's sight, I let my tidal wave of emotions release. Boiling rage. Gut-wrenching sadness. Gripping fear. The powerful emotions swirled inside me, threatening to consume my soul. My lip trembled. My nails dug into my palms. And my heart quivered.

Just when I thought I would burst into a million fragmented pieces, I was engulfed by three sets of arms. Warmth, calmness, and coolness all surrounded me in a dragon-sized hug. They sensed my emotions, overwhelming them as much as they did me. My head came to rest on one of their chests—Issik's, judging by the frigid aura.

What would I do without them?

I never wanted to find out.

Lifting my chin, I met each one of their gazes. "We need to do something."

"We will. This isn't the end. A minor setback," Jase assured me, but he wasn't hearing me. I was talking about right now.

"Tianna thinks she's hurt us. She's wrong," I vowed with conviction.

Curiosity entered Zade's eyes. "Did you learn something new in the Mirrored Shallows?"

I relaxed my fighting stance. "Uh, not exactly."

"Then there really isn't anything for us to do at the moment. I suggest you get some sleep. You look like you're going to crumble to the floor."

My shoulders straightened to prove Jase, the know-it-all, wrong. There was still some energy left in this body. If they weren't willing to do anything right now, then I would. Couldn't they see we didn't have time to waste?

Brushing past Issik, I stalked down the hall, heading away from my room and toward the stairs. The descendants might not let me leave the castle, but there were many, many rooms in Viperus Keep left to be explored. The woman in white had said the stones returned to a place of importance and meaning, to the heart of Viperus. Maybe that meant somewhere in this maze of a castle.

"Where are you going?" Issik asked, falling in step behind me. Zade was right beside him.

I kept walking, not that I actually thought I would get far.

The descendants were, if anything, predictable. Zade's blazing arms came around me, and swooped me off my feet. "The only place you are going is to bed, Little Gem."

"Let me go," I ordered, torn between crying and screaming.

Thick, contoured muscle kept me secured against Zade's chest, and I gave up fighting fairly quickly. I was too tired. Too weak. And outnumbered. Not to mention, in pain. I groaned as the slashes on my back made themselves known. Crap. I'd forgotten about my own injuries.

"You're hurt," Zade murmured, carefully putting me back on my feet. He lifted my shirt.

From the corner of my eye, I saw Issik's hands bunch into fists, and his expression freeze over. "I'm going to kill her," he snarled in a voice so low I almost didn't hear him.

"Get in line," Zade growled. "She will pay for this."

Wiggling Kieran's tattered shirt back down over the cuts, I kept my face neutral to block them from seeing the pain. "It's a few scratches. They'll heal."

"And we can help. You'll feel better after you've slept," the fire-breathing dragon reasoned. "Jase?" Zade called.

I let out a string of colorful f-bombs, knowing exactly what was coming. Zade had his hands on my shoulders and spun me around. Jase was waiting for me.

Son of a bitch.

Not again.

My head shook back and forth. "Don't you dare open your mouth," I hissed.

His violet eyes bore into mine. "Cupcake, calm down before you hurt yourself more."

"If you do this, I won't ever forgive you," I seethed, narrowing my eyes at the tranquility dragon who was about to force me to sleep.

Bringing his face near mine, his fingers tucked a

strand of hair behind my ear. "Sorry, Cupcake." Regret shimmered in his gaze, and I actually believed he was sorry for what he was about to do. Pain radiated from him, as if hurting me hurt him.

Poof. A cloud of purple smoke expelled from his kiss-able lips, except in this moment, I would have rather bit him than kissed him.

I woke up sweating my tits off, like my skin was melting off my body. Only one explanation came to mind, and no, it wasn't my hormones.

Zade.

God, he was hot. In more ways than just his body temperature.

Rolling my head to the side, I inspected my bed partner. Some girls might disapprove of waking up next to a different guy each day of the week. Not me. I enjoyed the variety, and I didn't really care what that said about me. Judgmental bitches could kiss my ass.

"How long have I been asleep?" I asked, stretching. I hated to admit that I *was* feeling better. The pain in my back was gone.

"Not long enough," Zade grumbled, yawning. "Do you know that you grind your teeth in your sleep?"

"It's better than drooling," I defended myself, rolling over onto my side. I doubted I'd ever get a normal night's sleep again. The descendants didn't seem to believe in a schedule.

His expression was thoughtful as his half-lidded eyes roamed over my face. "You're not mad," he stated, feeling my emotions.

Throwing off the covers, I contemplated whether or not I should also take off my shirt. Someone had removed Kieran's and slipped a clean one on me. Beads of sweat rolled between my breasts. "I'm too hot to be mad, but I still plan on killing Jase, by the way."

Zade's lips split into a grin. "I'm looking forward to it."

"I should give him a dose of his own medicine," I mumbled. My brain started to imagine all the ways I could get Jase back for knocking me out last night.

Zade moved closer, lifting up on his elbow so he was propped over me. "I'm supposed to bring you downstairs now that you're awake, but first…" His finger traced over my jaw, leaving trails of fire behind, and yet my face turned into his touch, craving more.

I was insane.

Dear God, is that all they ever thought about—kissing me? I wouldn't normally complain, but what I needed was a blast of Issik to counter the heat from Zade. "If you kiss me right now, I'm afraid I might spontaneously combust. It's so hot in here. Where's Issik?"

Hurt splashed into his eyes, but he blinked, quickly masking it. It hadn't been my intention to cause him pain or reject him.

"Shit. Sorry," Zade cursed, sitting up. He ran a hand over his face before climbing out of bed, and crossing the room to open a window. "I wasn't thinking," he admitted. His was back was to me as he leaned against the windowsill. "When I'm with you, it is so easy to forget you're human."

I got out of bed and padded across the room, berating myself for being so careless with his feelings. Laying a hand on his shoulder, I endured the wave of heat. Zade was worth being burned. "I didn't mean it to sound as if I preferred Issik over you. That's not the case. The truth is I have feelings for all of you. I don't want to hurt any of you."

Zade turned around and looked down at me. "This thing between the five of us is new. It will take some getting used to. And I'll try to remember to turn down the heat." He winked.

My shoulders relaxed, and I beamed up at him.

"We should probably find the others," he added, breaking the silent conversation we'd been having with our looks and smiles.

I was eager to see how Kieran was faring. Had his injuries completely healed?

Zade waited for me to toss on some clothes, before ushering me downstairs into the conservatory, a room made entirely out of glass. Kieran and Jase were sitting around a rectangular wooden table. Issik was standing, leaning against one of the glass walls. The sky was still gloomy and gray, casting somberness over the room. The conversation died when Zade and I walked in, making me suspicious. They were definitely hiding something from me, and it was time someone told me what the hell was going on here.

I brushed up against Issik, letting his natural coolness seep into my skin. He shot me a funny look.

My brow lifted. Was it so hard to believe I would pick him to stand next to? My critical gaze evaluated Kieran. Although he lounged in the chair with his usual carefree attitude, something felt wrong. His eyes lacked some of their luster, and his skin appeared paler.

Issik's hand landed on the small of my back, and the earth tilted underneath me as a gust of cold danced down my spine.

"Is someone going to say something, or are we just going to stare at each other?" I asked when no one began conversing.

Jase looked like a king at the head of the table. It wasn't even his house and yet it was clear which of the descendants was in charge. "Have you forgiven me?"

I frowned, my attention pulled away from Kieran, and coming to rest on the tranquility dragon. "Oh, I'll get you back, Jase Dior. When you least expect it."

"That's what I was worried about," he mumbled.

Issik's lips twitched as he loomed over me. "The witch isn't going to make this easy."

Jase tapped his fingers on top of the table, contemplating some scary-ass plan, I was sure. "When does she ever?"

"God, I can't wait to kill her," Zade added, the red in his eyes overtaking the soft brown.

Issik's scowl deepened, and darkness seemed to gather around him. "Get in line."

Jase stood up, pacing the length of the room. "We've

wasted enough time. Going to the Mirrored Shallows cost us." That was an understatement.

"What are we going to do?" I asked.

An unrecognizable emotion swept through his violet eyes, and it worried me. "Comb every inch of Viperus if we have to. We split up and section off the kingdom. Every day we get out there—rain or shine."

My arms crossed over my chest. "Great. Now that we have that out of the way, what are you guys keeping from me?"

Four sets of guarded eyes met mine. "What are you talking about, Cupcake?"

"I know there is something you're not telling me. I can feel it."

No one jumped at the opportunity to fill me in on their secret. Suddenly, they had a keen interest in the grain of the wood table, or the texture of the stone floors.

I engaged my bitch mode. "Don't ignore me! I don't need to be coddled."

"We don't want to worry you," Jase eventually answered, his palms flattened on the table as he leaned on its corner.

"About what?"

Their discomfort was evident. Issik sighed beside me, iciness infiltrating the air. "She is going to find out sooner or later. What is the point in prolonging it?"

Jase's gaze went around the room, looking at each descendant. One by one, they nodded. A decision had been made. Finally, those eyes reached mine. "Our powers are getting weaker," he revealed.

My mouth dropped open. To me, they were nearly

invincible. It was hard to imagine the four of them being anything but fearless, powerful dragons. "You didn't think that was something important I should know?"

The muscles in Jase's jaw tightened. "It isn't easy to admit, and we weren't entirely certain."

"Not until last night," Kieran added.

Meaning when he was struck down from the sky. From what I understood about the descendants, they weren't immortal, but nearly impossible to kill in their dragon form. They had healing abilities, and their scales were almost impenetrable, protecting their bodies from damage of all kinds—including a fall that would have killed a human. Something had been wrong with Kieran. This only reassured me that my hunch had been right, and that I had a valid reason to be so worried about him.

"As the deadline nears, we can feel the abilities inside us losing potency," Zade admitted in vexation.

Fan-flipping-tastic. Like we didn't have enough to stress about. It had seemed like an incredibly difficult task before, but doable. Now without them at full power to ward off Tianna's attacks, it felt hopeless.

"And you're afraid that if we don't find the stones soon, you'll be unable to defend yourselves against Tianna?"

Issik hooked a finger under my chin, lifting my face up to his. "It isn't just that. We wouldn't be able to protect you."

I swallowed. "You guys have to stop worrying about me. I'm not useless anymore. I have powers of my own."

It was all true, but none of us actually believed I could

take care of myself. I wasn't a superhero. I wasn't ridiculously smart. I wasn't immortal.

I was average.

Jase straightened up, his expression shifting. "You might be on to something."

I didn't like the sudden lightbulb I saw go off in his mind. "I should have kept my mouth shut," I grumbled.

"Definitely," Issik agreed.

Jase ignored us, moving forward with his brilliant thought. "We're going to train you."

My brows scrunched together. "Train me for what? And when do I have time for that?"

"We'll make time. You learning to defend yourself might be what helps us stay alive."

Issik scratched the day-old stubble under his chin. "That isn't a horrible idea."

My eyes darted from one descendant to the next, unable to believe any of them thought this was an answer to our problems. "Are you guys insane? Have you been paying attention at all since I got here?"

"She has a point," Kieran spoke up, having spent most of the time quietly listening. "What if she hurts herself... or worse?"

The "worse" being I accidentally kill myself, which wasn't out of the realm of possibility. "Finally, someone who understands me."

"Olivia is often a danger to herself." Kieran shot me a faint smile.

Jase wasn't about to let the idea go. "I think it could make a difference. We can add it to your tranquility training."

My body sunk against Issik, recognizing I was outnumbered, as always. On the flipside, I could use my new combat skills to kick their asses. That was a perk I couldn't say no to. "Fine. It's your grave, Dimples."

Jase chuckled. If I didn't know better, I would have thought he was looking forward to it.

Regardless of my argument that Kieran needed to stay behind and rest, the five of us were hoofing it through the woods to another creepy grave site on the west side of Viperus. The never-ending search for the Star of Poison continued. As a kid, I used to love hide-and-seek, but now, the game grew tiresome.

Kieran and I hadn't said much to each other since the night in Mirrored Shallows, but a charge of electricity hummed between us. I swore he was playing with his lip on purpose to taunt me with his sexiness. I remembered all too well what it was like to have the cool metal touching me in the most intimate places.

My cheeks flushed. Christ, I was suddenly wearing too many clothes. "Stop looking at me like that," I hissed between my teeth, keeping my voice low so the others wouldn't hear me.

"I don't know what you're talking about," he replied as if he was an innocent lamb. His fingers brushed mine, and I jerked my hand away, afraid the others would pick up on something, but the light touch had done its damage, heightening the color in my face.

I scowled at the poison dragon, giving him a pointed

glare. Didn't know what I was talking about my left butt cheek. I was on to him, and he had another thing coming if he thought he could seduce me in the woods with the others present. "I am not some prize you can claim."

"Is that why you didn't want me to tag along? Because you're afraid they would see how you feel about me, how I can make your body come alive?" he murmured near my ear, causing my belly to flip.

Maybe Kieran needed to realize he wasn't the only dragon who could make my blood sing. He might not be so cocky then, and once the thought took root, a reckless idea took shape.

We had caught Zade's attention with our odd behavior. "What is up with the two of you? he asked, as we stumbled upon a clearing in the dense forest. "What's with the whispering and keeping secrets? You're both acting so weird."

Jase and Issik, who had been trailing behind, paused with the rest of us. "We are not," Kieran and I said at the same time, making us look that much more suspicious. We were going to have to tell the others what had happened in the cave eventually.

I preferred to do it later. Much later. When we weren't at the cusp of a spooky-ass grave. The area we stood in was filled with carved headstones, scattered across the grounds like the gravedigger had been drunk.

But Jase wouldn't let it go.

He eyed Kieran and me with intense scrutiny, which made me squirm with unease. "No, something definitely happened between the two of you."

"Knowing Kieran, he probably seduced her," Issik

added in an offhand comment, but that was all it took to light a spark.

Jase's gaze was pure violet fire as he zeroed in on Kieran. "Tell me you didn't."

Kieran did the worst thing possible. He grinned.

Suddenly, Kieran was on the ground with Zade on top of him. I stood on the sidelines, nibbling my lip, and pondering if I should do or say something. Instead, I let them beat the shit out of each other. If the others weren't going to do anything, then screw it, neither was I.

Neanderthal dragons.

Would they ever learn fists didn't solve everything?

Zade's lip bled down his chin, and Kieran's knuckles were cut open when they finally broke apart and shoved to their feet.

"I didn't plan it, okay? It just happened. What was I supposed to do? Ignore her emotions? I can't help it you got anger instead of love. It probably has something to do with your temper."

I had to agree, but Zade didn't. The hotheaded dragon moved like lightning, grabbing Kieran by the shirt, and I thought for sure we were in for round two.

"Cool off," Jase ordered, intervening before any more fists were thrown. About damn time. "We're here for the stone. We can discuss Olivia's sex life later."

My mouth dropped open. "Hell no. No one is discussing my sex life—now or later." It was like I was invisible.

"Are you saying she picked you?" Zade challenged Kieran, flames licking in his crimson eyes. This wasn't a competition, and Kieran wasn't the winner, however much that twisted smirk on his lips said otherwise.

I cleared my throat. "I'm not picking anyone," I insisted, ready to change the topic to safer ground—like the stone. I might as well have been talking to a brick wall. No one listened to me.

It was time to take action.

Walking up to Issik—the only one who hadn't said anything—I placed my hands on his shoulders and lifted up to my toes. Before he guessed what I had planned, I sealed my lips to his in a glacial kiss like the first frost. I molded into him, sinking into his body.

From the moment my lips touched his, all I could think about was why it had taken me so long to kiss him. My fingers burrowed into his silky blond hair that came to his jawline. His taste was cool, minty, and addicting. My mouth tingled as his tongue parted my lips to dip inside. His cool caress against my tongue was refreshing, and I craved more.

My spine arched, seeking the comfort of his touch, and I wasn't disappointed. Issik's hands slid to my hips, pulling me against the length of him. A tender breath escaped my lips, as I succumbed to the heady persuasion of his mouth. What was meant to be a quick kiss had gained the power to snowball. It scared me—the ability the descendants had to make me tremble with desire at their feet.

And tremble I did.

A shiver rippled through me.

Issik slowly broke off the kiss to look at me with bright eyes that lit up in the dark. An emotion flickered through the need churning in his stormy, light blue gaze. Could it be hurt? "Why did you do that?" he asked in a strained voice.

I eyed him intently, wondering how I had hurt him. My fingers lightly traced the hard planes on his face, and I watched the way his irises darkened under my touch. "Because I wanted to."

"Good." His tone held a warning, but his arms were pulling me closer. "We're not finished yet."

We weren't?

Closing the distance between us, he fastened his lips over mine a second time. Pure white heat shot through me, tightening the lower part of my body.

"Enough," rumbled Jase. He slipped his hands around my arms, separating me from Issik. "We don't have time for this."

I blinked, giving myself a few moments to catch my breath, and when the ground was solid under my feet, I directed my gaze at Kieran. "Did you feel that?"

A deep frown marred his face. "You made your point."

With a slightly unsteady hand, I smoothed my tousled hair. "Like I told you before, I can't choose. The four of you are going to have to find a way to deal with that."

"You guys need to get your hormones in check, and stop thinking with your dicks. We have more pressing matters at hand." Jase rubbed his temples in exasperation.

"Hear! Hear!"

Jase shot me a raised brow, and I realized my snarky agreement hadn't been inside my head. "You're not helping either. Keep your lips to yourself. No more kissing anyone until we find the stone."

"Who died and made you king?"

Jase's jaw worked. "My father."

Ugh. I hated it when he was so literal, but it didn't stop the guilt. A parent's death was nothing to joke about. No one knew that better than me, and it didn't matter if it had been a month, a year, or a hundred years; the pain stayed with you.

Releasing me, he barked out orders. "Same drill as before. Split up. Find the stone. Stop the curse."

Without waiting to hear who would be assigned as my protector, I took off into the misty graveyard. There were times being surrounded by the descendants was over-whelming. They each had such powerful personalities and an enticing presence. My body didn't know what it wanted when the four of them were near.

I could feel Issik behind me. Hovering. One dragon I could handle, even the coldest of the bunch. My lips were still tingling from our kiss, and I touched my bottom lip, losing focus once again on why I was in a graveyard.

The wind picked up, blowing through the leaves and branches before tossing back my hair. Inside the whistling of the cool air, I heard a voice. It was trying to tell me something.

My entire body froze as I stretched to listen.

It's a trap.

Spinning around, I found Issik right beside me. "Did you hear that?" I whispered.

"I don't hear anything," he replied in a normal volume, scanning the area around us.

Lifting a finger into the air, I shushed him and waited, listening to see if I would hear it again. The wind did not disappoint. *Leave. You must go. Before it is too late.*

My eyes swept over the graveyard. "Someone is sending us a warning."

Issik's muscles tensed, and his mouth thinned into a straight line. "You're sure?"

I wrapped my arms around myself and nodded. "Pretty sure." The wind had died down, taking the whisperings with it, and leaving me a mess.

A spear of lightning lanced across the sky, making his face look sinister as he shifted into protector mode. "The sooner we find this stone, the closer I'll be to killing this witch."

Thunder cracked close to our location, and I couldn't

help but think Tianna was responding to Issik's threat. I panicked, remembering the last time lightning had struck. My hands fisted into the material of Issik's shirt. "We need to get out of here. Now, Issik," I pleaded.

His arms came around me. "Hey, it's going to be okay."

My head shook. "You don't know that. This feels wrong."

With a tenderness he rarely showed, Issik ran his fingers over my hair. "Your fear is so strong, but you can't let it rule you. I need you to be brave. Can you do that?"

Inspired by the vibrant determination on his face, I nodded. Courage was the resistance of fear. I had read that once on a fortune cookie, and the words couldn't have been truer at this moment. I needed courage. It was the only way I could stand against the witch.

Hesitating, he laced his fingers through mine, keeping me close. "Good." Together we continued our exploration of the tombs.

"How did you win babysitting duty?" I asked, trying to take my mind off the fact that we were undoubtedly all walking into some kind of witch web.

"Because Jase thinks I'm the least likely to seduce you in a cemetery," he replied with the slightest traces of sarcasm.

I snorted under my breath, but a little louder than I had meant. Did that mean Jase didn't trust himself alone with me either? "He should be more worried about me making a move on you."

A smile tugged at Issik's lips. "My sentiments exactly."

In the dark, it wasn't easy to search for an object as small as the Star of Poison. I hadn't understood at first why the descendants thought the burial grounds would be a likely place to find the stone. Not until I noticed the detail in a few of the headstones, particularly the ones that were nearly as tall as me. Besides ornate designs and beautiful symbols I couldn't interpret, many had jewels and other valuables encrusted into the stone or placed inside cavities.

"Does each kingdom have their own burial sites?" I was thinking if I had to spend the next few months rummaging among the dead, I might need to perform a few cleansing rituals.

"Not like these. We all have our own way of dealing with those who have passed on. Kieran's tradition buries the deceased, Zade's burns them, and Jase's releases them to the sea."

"And you?" I prompted.

Issik unwound his fingers from mine and jammed his hands into his pockets. "We freeze the bodies under sheets of ice."

I shuddered.

"Are you cold?" he asked, concern crinkling the corners of his eyes.

"No, not really. It's this place. It gives me the heebie-jeebies."

"There's nothing to be afraid of."

He received one of my bullshit glares. *Be brave*, I reminded myself.

Issik's massive shoulders gave a shrug. "Okay, so I lied, but I want you to feel safe with me."

"I do," I reassured him because he looked as if he needed it. My hand reached out to touch his arm.

"No touching!" Jase's voice carried from the other side of the clearing. The mist was too dense for me to see him clearly, but I could tell he was glowering.

I rolled my eyes. "We should make out just to piss him off more."

Issik's brows inched up. "It might mean a death sentence for me, but I'm game if you are."

Grinning, I walked around a triangular piece of stone in the ground, moving away from the temptation of Issik. What was I going to do with them?

That was a problem for another day, because a headstone a few feet in front of me captured my attention. I squinted, needing to make sure I wasn't seeing things I wanted to be there. Moving closer through the evening mist, I saw a sparkle of green under the moon's glow, causing my heart to batter in my chest.

In a kneejerk reaction, my hand shot out, grabbing Issik on the forearm. "Tell me you see that." It was comparable in size and shape to the Star of Tranquility, but as we drew nearer, a nervous feeling pitted in my gut.

"If you're talking about the hunk of emerald, then yes."

"Do you think…?"

His head angled to the side. "Only one way to find out."

With my heart in my throat and gobs of nerves shaking my steps, we walked to the tomb. I reached out, letting my fingers wrap around the smooth crystal. I waited for the jolt of magic, but in my heart, I knew this wasn't the Star of Poison. Nothing happened, and disappointment crushed my soul.

Lifting my gaze to meet Issik's, my shoulders slumped. "This isn't the star."

"No. That is not a star," he confirmed.

Following the setback, a fresh bout of frustration hit me. I chucked the crystal across the yard into the thick fog blanketing the clearing. "This blows," I huffed, letting my irritation leak out of me.

Something resembling alarm came into Issik's eyes, and my stomach muscles clenched. "Olivia, we need to go."

"What did I—"

Issik reached for me, slipped a hand onto the small of my back, and applied pressure, urging me back the way we'd come, but a movement caught my attention in my peripheral vision. My heels dug in, and my head whipped to the side. It wouldn't have mattered if I had kept walking or not, because all hell broke loose.

Literally.

Bodies rose from the graves. Wait. That wasn't quite right. They weren't physical bodies, but wisps of the humans they'd once been. Ghosts.

Holy rising dead!

My mouth hung on the ground at the sight, and Issik tugged on my hand. "What is happening?"

"Tianna is waking up the dead," Issik stated matter-of-factly, like it was as normal as rain falling.

"She can do that?" I screeched, drawing the ghosts' attention.

Issik's hand clamped over my mouth, and he pulled me to him. "Yes, she can," his frosty voice whispered in my ear. "And if you don't want those ghosts to try and possess you, keep quiet."

Good advice. I should take it, and I would take it.

And yet my innate concern for the others overruled my own safety. "What about Zade, Kieran, and Jase? We have to warn them."

Issik stiffened like a steel rod had been jammed into his spine. "They can take care of themselves. What we need to do is get you out of here."

I debated with myself while Issik steered us through the graveyard—run with Issik to safety, or turn and warn the other descendants? Maybe it was the shock from seeing a scene straight out of a horror film, but something inside me snapped. My brows drew together, and I yanked my hand free from Issik's. Before he had a chance to capture me again, I spun around, my hair fanning out in the air, and took off, running straight toward the gang of hovering ghosts.

"Son of a bitch," I heard Issik swear, followed by the pounding of his feet.

This might be a stupid idea, but I had to try. What was the point of having powers if I couldn't use them for good, like saving my dragons? No more chickening out for me.

I would fight.

Knowing I only had a second until Issik caught me, I opened my mouth and released a stream of tranquility from deep within my chest. The haze of purple swirled and twirled around the gang of ghosts.

Hell yes. Take that, you dead bastards.

I was a badass… for five whole seconds.

The mist began to dissipate, and instead of the spirits dropping off into a deep sleep, they shook off the dazing effect, and homed their blank gazes in on me.

"Shit. Shit. Shit. Why didn't that work?" I mumbled, backing up into a wall that turned out to be Issik.

His fingers were at my waist, keeping me from toppling over. "Because they're already asleep—an eternal sleep."

"That would have been nice to know beforehand." Our window of escape was gone, and I was to blame. Tianna's cackle echoed throughout the graveyard.

Issik shoved me behind him, taking a stand against the ghosts. Tingles danced in the air between us, indicating a shift was in the making. I backed up to give him room, and a hand touched my shoulder. I got a bad feeling along with a chill that was very different than Issik's.

Don't turn around. Don't do it, my mind chanted, but my body was already in motion.

A silent scream lodged in my esophagus.

The ghost in front of me wore a top hat, but that wasn't the strange part. He gave me a wobbly grin before he floated into me.

"Olivia!" Issik bellowed, but it was too late.

I'd been possessed by a mother-freaking ghost.

The coldness in my chest intensified, and I became a prisoner in my own body. My thoughts and feelings were mine, but someone else controlled my arms and legs. Unable to stop what was happening, my mouth opened, and the spirit delivered a message.

Deliver the stones, or I'll kill her.

Damn. Could my voice have sounded any freakier? I

would have nightmares for years. Being possessed was certainly not something I would recommend. Not even once. Nothing else the Veil could do to me would shake me as badly as this had.

When the soul left my body, it felt like someone had a giant suction cup on my heart and then released the pressure, freeing me from its tormented possession. Trying to catch my breath, I sunk to my knees. Dirt and gravel dug into my flesh, but I didn't feel the pain.

In fact, I felt nothing.

I was empty.

No emotion. No thoughts. Just a black hole.

"Olivia!" Issik shook my shoulders. His eyes were filled with terror, and I could tell that it hadn't been the first time he'd shouted my name.

I blinked, feeling as if I'd awakened from a brush with death, and was amazed to be alive.

His fingers roamed over my face. "Is it you?"

Needle pinpricks radiated over my skin, starting with my toes and traveling to my head. It was the feeling you get after sitting on your foot for too long. My body was waking back up.

"It's me," I assured him.

He yanked me into his arms, pulling me into a tight embrace. "Little Warrior," he said it like an answer to prayer.

An odd noise, between a curse and a sob, left my lips. My forehead pressed to his chest. "I might be sick. God, I really hate throwing up."

Cool fingers took hold of my chin and tipped my face upward. "You're so pale, and your nose is bleeding."

My hand flew to my nose and wiped under it. Sticky red blood covered my fingers. The sight made me woozy. "I need a minute. Don't let me go." I shivered, my body not yet recovered fully from the possession of the spirit.

"You're cold." His fingers moved to rub up and down my arms in an effort to chase away the cold, which for him was a futile motion. "We need to find Zade." Issik bent down, scooping me up in his arms.

I could definitely use some of Zade's heat. "It's not you." I needed to explain the chattering of my teeth, so he wouldn't take it personally. "The ghost… he was so cold inside me." The air from my lungs came out in a white puff.

"A side effect from being possessed. It will pass, but quicker with Zade's help." His long legs ate up the ground.

My head rested on Issik's firm shoulder. The ghosts were wandering aimlessly; they no longer seemed interested in me since having delivered their message. Still, I doubted it was good for the Veil to have a bunch of dead running amok. They needed to be dealt with soon.

"What happened?" demanded a voice I recognized as Jase's. He was always demanding.

Issik handed me off to Zade, and I gladly entered his furnace. "She was possessed. Warm her up while I take care of the restless dead."

Nothing more needed to be said. The fire dragon spun me around to face him, his fingers coming to frame my blue cheeks. As his lips descended to mine, I caught a flash of Issik shifting. My eyes fluttered shut at the first touch of Zade's kiss. Warmth blazed back into me. From one extreme to the other, my body temperature flipped, now burning like the core of the sun. I felt as if I was glowing from the inside out.

"Better?" he asked after pulling back.

"Much," I agreed.

"I swear I don't know what we did around here for fun before you."

The snarky comment died on my lips, as I noticed a dragon missing. Where the heck was Kieran? I turned my attention back to the graveyard, searching for Issik. Jase and Zade stood shoulder to shoulder next to me, boxing me in with their tall bodies, which was obviously a protective maneuver in case another ghost decided to invade my body.

What was Issik doing? Sacrificing himself as a diversion? There were too many. How was he going to fight them all? I couldn't let him do it. I needed him as much as I did the others.

My blood pressure rose. "Are you guys going to just stand here?"

"Kieran is with him… somewhere," Jase answered.

The thick fog made it really difficult to see for any distance. "Great, you sent the wounded dragon to help."

Jase tilted his chin down to look at me. "You're more important than Issik or Kieran."

Frustration tore through me, only to be entangled by the strands of worry piling up in my stomach.

Issik circled overhead, dipping low over the clearing. Slivers of ice expelled from his chest, and the frost encased the ghostly forms, freezing them on the spot. Zade reacted. Wrapping me in his arms, he protected me from the cold, his body exuding an insane amount of heat, but it did the trick.

Teamwork at its finest.

The ground shook when Issik landed. A dozen ghost popsicles were scattered over the cemetery. *Swoosh.* His tail swung in an arc, taking out half of the ice statues and shattering them to little bits. The sky rained shards of their ghostly souls. He repeated the movement until every last one was gone.

I exhaled, breathing easily. "Can we go home now?" I asked, sinking against Zade. "I've had enough *fun* for today."

"There's always tomorrow," he replied with a smile.

"That's what I'm afraid of."

14

Tempers grew shorter every day. A week passed. The days drained away, and the dreams became a nightly occurrence since the possession. I didn't know what that witch had done to me, but I didn't like it. She could take her voodoo ways and shove them where the sun don't shine. And she could take the dreams back too. I was done with the restless nights, the torment, and the stress of it all.

Maybe that was part of her plan—to drive me mad.

Well, it was working.

This particular night, I had another one of my strange dreams, but it was different than the others; it broke through to reality.

A woman with wavy hair the color of wheat, that cascaded down her back stood in my room. Her eyes were milky and pale, hiding their true color. I didn't know why that particular detail stood out to me, but it seemed important somehow—like it would reveal her identity.

Crazy, I know.

But what dreams weren't? They never made any sense. It

was as if my subconscious constantly wanted to fuck with me, but in this case, it was a witch.

The woman glided across the floor like someone from a horror movie, her tattered dress dragging on the ground. I scooted back in the bed, tempted to throw the covers over my eyes, and start humming to myself.

"You're not crazy," she whispered to me, except her mouth never opened. Her words projected into the air.

I tugged the blanket up to my chin, noticing for the first time I was alone. No dragon snored beside me. "I'm not sure how much weight that holds coming from a ghost in a dream."

This island was schizophrenic.

Some ghosts wanted to help me. Others wanted to possess me. What did she want? Was she a ghost? Was she someone important? Or a follower of Tianna? She could, of course, be a product of my colorful imagination.

"I'm not a ghost per se. More of a guide."

My heart beat so fast in my chest I thought I was going to be sick. "You're the woman from the cave?"

She nodded as her fingers played with a gold locket around her neck. "The stone is closer than you think."

She had my undivided attention. I tossed the covers aside and sat straight up. "Can you tell me where it is? I'm desperate."

"It is not far from the eye."

"Whose? Mine?" I frantically searched the room, looking for something to clue me in on where the star might be. Was it here in my bedroom? It couldn't be that simple.

She snuck up on me while I scrutinized every inch of my space, and finding her suddenly so close to my face startled me. I let out a little squeak of surprise, instantly concerned she might try to possess me. I stayed perfectly still, but ready to fight.

Her fingers reached for the back of her neck, unclasping the necklace she wore. "I want you to have this. Let it be the light to guide you through the darkness."

Did she mean figuratively or literally?

Holding the chain, she moved toward me, and I stayed motionless as she wrapped the necklace around my neck, fastening the clasp. The charm dangled between my breasts. I touched the gold locket and found it to be warm.

"I don't know what to say. Thank you?" My eyes lifted to meet hers.

The room had suddenly been sucked of all light. No moonlight filtered through the curtains. No candle burned on the small desk in the corner. Nothing but darkness and the sound of my heavy breathing filled the room. The woman jerked away from the bed and fluttered back and forth through the room. Her white dress was the only way I could track her movements.

Crawling to the end of the bed, I followed her sporadic pacing with my eyes. "What's wrong?"

"She's coming." Her voice had gone soft and scary.

"Who?"

Her eyes flew to the door, and she came to a harsh halt. "The witch. You must wake up. Now!"

Easier said than done. I couldn't just snap my fingers and boom I was awake. What was I supposed to do? Scrambling to lay back down, I closed my eyes. Wake up. Wake up. Wake up, I chanted. Regardless of the panic rising within me, I remained stuck in the dream, awaiting whatever horror Tianna had planned for me.

Hiss. Hiss. Hiss.

God. No. Please don't let that be what I think it is.

Everyone has fears. The one thing that makes them lose their shit—heights, spiders, blood. Mine was snakes.

I fucking hated snakes.

More than lima beans. More than winter. More than being homeless.

I got that a viper was Viperus's mascot, but that didn't mean I was thrilled to live in a castle with a snake carved into it. Yet, when it came to the dragon that lived in it, I would do anything to save him and the others, including dealing with a deranged witch... and her pets.

The vicious, venomous viper slithered across my floor like he owned the room. I didn't know when the woman in white had vanished, but she was no longer here, leaving me all alone with a brood of snakes. One after another, they slunk under the door, through the windows, and any other hole they could squeeze into with ease.

It might have been a trick of my mind or one of Tianna's hexes, but hidden in the hissing that echoed in the room was a voice. I was damn sure snakes didn't talk or, at the very least, they weren't supposed to.

Tick tock goes the clock. Ding-dong the key is dead.

Are you kidding me? Nursery rhymes? I had to still be dreaming. And they got the last line wrong. It was "the witch is dead."

In a puff of smoke, the nightmare faded.

I bolted upright in bed, cold sweat glistening over my body. The air in my lungs came out in quick short pants while I caught my breath. I told myself I was okay. Nothing could hurt me. But that feeling of security lasted a split second.

A shadow on the floor drew my gaze, and like my dream, darkness slithered over the wood planks. The dream might have faded, but the snakes had remained. They climbed up the side of the bed, forked tongues tasting the air.

A scream ripped from my throat.

Jase jumped out of bed like the castle was on fire. The bed sheet tangled around his legs, giving him a Greek toga vibe. In another situation, I would have appreciated the look on him—golden skin, tight abs, and eyes that glowed in the dark. Yeah, Jase Dior was definitely a rare breed of male.

"Get back on the bed," I yelped, thinking the snakes would bite him.

His body was rigid as he waited for an attack that never came. "What's wrong?" His sharp eyes ran over the room, trying to pinpoint the threat.

"Don't you see them? The s-snakes?" My voice tripped over the word. I refused to peek over the edge of the bed.

He raked a hand through his hair. "I don't see anything, Cupcake. It must have been a nightmare."

Oh, I didn't doubt I had been locked in a room of horror, but when that hellish room became reality, that was when you had a problem. Jase wasn't going to be able to convince me that what I had seen hadn't been real. The witch was toying with me.

Did that mean I was close to finding the key?

Or was she, in her sick way, trying to motivate me?

I curled up on the bed, hugging my knees. "I'm so tired. She won't let me sleep," I murmured, rocking back and forth.

Jase hiked the sheet up, freeing his legs, and climbed back into bed. "You mean Tianna?"

"Unless Harlow suddenly developed the ability to torture me in my dreams."

"Funny." His lips twitched as he gathered my distraught body into his arms. "The others have noticed the restlessness you've been suffering at night. Do you want me to help?"

For once, I was tempted by tranquility, but I shook my head. I didn't want to sleep. "Could you hold me instead?" Somehow my brain concluded I would be safer in his arms, as if he could chase her away.

"I thought you'd never ask." He settled back down, propping his head on the pillow and opening an arm.

Without hesitation, I nestled against him, resting my face in the space between his neck and shoulder. The tension and fear lingering from the nightmare began to clear. "Don't get any ideas and try that tranquility crap on me," I muttered.

His fingers ran through my hair. "Are you sure? A good night's sleep devoid of dreams might be what you need."

Under my hand, his heart beat steadily, and it comforted me, feeling his source of life, but a dark cloud nagged at the back of my head. *For how long?* it pestered. I didn't want to think about that. Not now. "This is better than sleep."

"Everything will be okay," Jase reassured, pressing a kiss to my forehead. "I promise."

How could he make such a statement? It might never be okay again. Without the stone, they would die. And then what? The last place I wanted to be was stranded on an exclusive island with a lunatic witch. None of us knew what would happen if the descendants died, but speculating about it wasn't going to change anything.

Sleep was out of the picture for the night, but wrapped up in Jase, I didn't mind. Lifting my head slightly, I saw the moonlight spill across the side of his face, illuminating his rugged sexiness, and I swore I heard the heavens sing.

"What are you wearing?"

The question every girl longed to hear. And Jase thought he had game. Hilarious. "Padding," I replied, patting the pillows strapped around my chest. "In case I fall."

Jase shook his head, clearly trying to figure out my madness. That made two of us. "I don't plan on beating the crap out of you."

"One can never be too prepared when I'm involved."

His eyes sparkled, and my belly squirmed in response. "Touché."

"Okay, I'm ready. Let's do this shit." Shit being self-defense or something like that. I'd been in a few fights, but I was talking about hair pulling and boob punching, nothing that required me to defend myself against wraiths and griffins. That was a new level I had yet to unlock.

Thick lashes framed his gorgeous violet eyes, and a slow grin pulled at the corners of his wicked mouth. The back of his knuckles feathered over my cheek, sending a thousand electrifying tingles over me. "You're almost too cute."

I blinked. Holy crap. A deep yearning that had been there since I laid eyes on him clawed at me. Jase had a way of leaving a stunning first impression. My head angled to the side as I regarded him. "Cute," I repeated, unable to stop my lips from curling. "You think this is cute?" I asked, my hand gesturing down my marshmallow torso.

He gave a slight shrug. "On you, it somehow works."

My hips rolled in the worst attempt at a stripper move. "I'm bringing sexy back." The words came out with a straight face, but it didn't last long before I busted out laughing. Sexy I was not.

"If you keep flirting with me, we're going to end up on the floor." His eyes roamed over my body.

This made me laugh more. Clutching my padded belly like Santa Claus, I tried to gain control of my laughter. "Are we really doing this?" I asked, glancing around the room. It had been cleared out with all the furniture pushed to one wall.

He stretched his arms out to the side and then over his head, his T-shirt lifting above his gym shorts to reveal his drool-worthy abs. "It's time for you to learn how to defend yourself. You didn't get padded up for nothing."

"Why do I need to learn? I have you for that." It had been a joke, but seeing the determination in Jase's face made me glad I'd gone the extra mile.

"Olivia," Jase scolded me in his no-nonsense voice. "It seems that no matter how much we try to protect you, Tianna finds ways to get to you. Last night is a prime example. You need to be strong mentally and physically."

Ugh. The snake dream. "Did you have to bring that up again?" I was doing everything within my power to pretend it had never happened.

"We can't let the witch get inside your head. Who knows what kind of damage she could do."

A shiver trickled down my spine at the idea of Tianna continually infiltrating my mind. My mind was a frightening enough place, without some vindictive witch getting her hands on it. It got me thinking though...

"What about the other girls? Do they know how to fight?" Maybe I wasn't the only one whom Tianna tortured with her mind games.

"Some of them, but most of them never had a reason to."

"I love being special."

Jase's lips twitched.

For the first half hour, Jase went over some basic footing and defensive techniques, which was honestly a waste of time and effort. I spent most of the time on the floor. It was embarrassing, but my balance was off-kilter with the extra padding. And Jase didn't help matters. The dragon could barely keep a straight face around me. This was the worst idea on the planet, but I wasn't a quitter. Jase moved on to lunging and attacking, luckily without any weapons, just getting used to the motions and learning the most effective moves for someone of my stature. I lacked the brute strength and towering height the descendants each possessed. He tossed in some tranquility lessons, testing my skill under pressure. That was the only test I passed.

But I did excel at falling on my ass and cursing.

"This has got to go," Jase said, pulling out my stuffing and tossing it behind him, all the while doing his best to retain his stern expression. The corners of his lips gave him away. They were dying to curl as he hovered over me. I was on the ground. Again. "I don't think I can watch you fall one more time. It's painful."

Lying flat on my back, I winced and sat up. "There is no way this is more painful for you than me."

He extended both his hands to help me to my feet. "Maybe we should try something else."

"You think?" I shot back, placing my hands in his, and with ease, he lifted me to my feet. It felt marvelous to be rid of the extra protection, like taking off my bra after a long day.

"Okay, smartass. Maybe this will grab your attention." Releasing my hands, he sauntered to the right corner of the room and bent down, picking up something wrapped in a cloth. He unraveled the material and straightened. As he started to turn around, I closed the space between us to see what he had been hiding.

My eyes popped out of my head at the first sight of the gold dagger, and I came to a jerky halt, nearly toppling over my own feet. "What the hell are you going to do with that?"

Jase flipped the blade in the air. "Teach you to use it."

I busted out laughing. "You want to give me a knife? Are you insane? What if I trip and fall on it?"

"She has a point." Issik's voice drifted in from the doorway, where he rested against the frame.

My hands went up in the air. "Thank you. Finally, a voice of reason."

"Issik, you're not helping. Don't you have something to do, like find a star?" Jase suggested between gritted teeth.

Issik gave a one-shoulder shrug. "Kieran and Zade went out."

I whipped my head toward Issik. "Without me?"

His eyes flicked to my face, but it was Jase who answered. "Afraid so, Cupcake."

I spun around, uncertain what I was feeling. Left out? I should have been glad they went out into the woods without me. All I'd done was complain about how tired I was, and yet, I was disappointed that I'd been left behind.

"Could you pick a different nickname? That one constantly makes me hungry," I snapped, feeling moody.

Jase lowered his lashes in a naughty look. "Me too."

Argh. They were devils. All four of them. The way their minds worked gave me whiplash.

Issik stepped into the room, breezing past me to stand in front of Jase. "This is why I'm staying. All anyone thinks about is seducing her."

"And you don't?" Jase challenged him.

"I didn't say that," Issik replied with a clenched jaw.

"Three *is* more fun than two." Did I say that out loud?
Crap.

What was wrong with my mouth? Why didn't it know when to shut up and keep things to myself? It was as if it had a mind of its own, spewing out whatever it pleased.

"Is that so?" Jase asked, tilting his head to the side. The two dragons stood shoulder-to-shoulder, eyeing me with twin quizzical expressions.

My fingers fumbled with the charm around my neck.

"It's the lack of sleep. It's making me delusional. I don't know what I'm saying anymore."

"Uh-huh."

Jase's eyes bounced between the weapon and me before narrowing. "Where did you get that necklace? It looks familiar."

"Um, the lady in my dream gave it to me." Truthfully, I'd completely forgotten about it until now.

Jase and Issik both choked. "What are we going to do with her?" Jase grumbled as he and Issik both moved to get a closer look at the charm.

Issik's cool fingers brushed along my skin, causing my breath to catch. "I've seen this before as well, but I can't recall on whose neck."

"Why did she give it to you?" Jase asked.

"She said something about it guiding me through darkness." My memory wasn't so good, not with the two of them clouding my senses.

Issik let the charm dangle back over my neck. "Do you think it is safe? What if it's one of Tianna's tricks?" he posed to Jase.

Why hadn't I thought of that? I glanced down at the circle pendant. In the center was an intricate filigree design. Could it be this was a cursed talisman? I didn't want to imagine what kind of heinous things it would do to me if it were, in fact, hexed.

Jase sighed, looking troubled. "More questions we don't have time to answer. I can't explain it, but I don't think there's any sorcery at play here."

Good enough for me, and Issik too it seemed. And Jase was right, we didn't have time for another mystery. The clock was ticking, which meant I needed to pull on my ninja pants and get this shit done. When Tianna came, which was only a matter of time, I wouldn't cower at her feet. I stretched my arm toward Jase. "Hand over the blade."

Issik stepped to the side, eyeing the gold dagger. "You take that blade, and there's no going back." He turned his icy glare to Jase and poked a finger into his chest. "You better hope no blood is shed, or I am holding you responsible."

Flipping the blade so the handle was held out for me to grab, Jase offered me the sharp weapon. "This won't kill a witch, but it will do some serious damage to griffins, imps, goblins, and other nasties who are under the witch's rule."

My fingers wrapped around the smooth hilt. "Good to know." I then rewound the conversation in my head. "Did you say goblins?"

"We have all kinds of nasties in the Veil to be wary of," Issik stated.

"Delightful," I said dryly.

By the end of the day, my skills had improved very little. I managed to avoid hurting anyone, including myself, but I couldn't say I had any actual ability wielding a dagger. Flinging the blade toward the wall, I watched as it clamored to the ground, not even making a dent. My shoulders slumped, and I let my arm hang heavily at my side. The weapon might seem light at first, but after an hour of swinging, jabbing, and stabbing, my arm was about to fall off.

"Let's face it. I suck."

Jase came up behind me and massaged my aching shoulders. "You'll get better with practice."

I rolled my neck and moaned. If he stopped, I might threaten him with the blade. "There's no time, Dimples. This is hopeless. I'm in so much trouble, aren't I?"

"Depends on what kind of trouble you're referring to. I've had to spend the entire day trying not to think about kissing you." His seductive voice murmured near my ear.

Issik ran a thumb over his bottom lip. "I know what you mean. It's torture keeping her safe, when all I want to do is sweep her off to the nearest bed."

I was unable to look away, caught in the storm swirling in Issik's eyes. "Now is not the time for sexual innuendos."

Issik grinned—actually grinned, the Ice Prince and my breath caught. "There is always time for sex."

What was happening? They got a little sweaty and their minds went off the deep end?

I found myself sandwiched between Issik and Jase, and my blood pressure skyrocketed. This was supposed to be a training session, but I had a feeling the only thing I *would* learn was how to handle two guys at once.

"Is this a test?" My voice took on a husky quality I didn't know I possessed.

Jase lifted the blond hair off the back of my neck, gathering it to the side and over my shoulder. "The question is whether you will pass."

Now this was a test I could get behind. My hands lifted and looped around Issik's neck. "Is that so?"

Neither of them kissed me on the lips. They each bent their heads and went for opposite sides of my neck. Tranquility and ice swirled, encompassing me in an addictive cocktail I couldn't stop sampling.

Holy dragon babies.

What had I gotten myself into?

Issik's tongue traced along the pulsing vein on my

throat, and I welcomed the sensations he created. I had been in a similar position before, just with a different mixture of dragons. What would it be like to try other combinations? My mind tumbled through the possibilities. Fire and ice. Poison and tranquility. Tranquility, Ice, and Fire. My math skills were on par with my combat skills, so I stopped trying to figure out the number of dragon mishmashes I could get myself into, and focused on what Jase and Issik's hands were doing to my body.

Issik had a rigid control I wanted to destroy; I wanted him to let loose, completely. I pressed every inch of my body into the full hardness of his, fisting my fingers into his hair. Pushing up onto my toes, I covered his lips with mine. Ice so cold it nearly stole my breath poured into my mouth, but I never faltered in our kiss. In fact, I took it further, letting him capture my low moan with his mouth.

"Fuck," he muttered, his fingers squeezing my bottom.

Victory.

It was sweet and oh so satisfying.

Issik spun me around, passing me to Jase, who was quick to pick up where Issik had left off. Jase claimed my lips with a hungry passion that nearly drove me straight over the edge. I wanted the release more than I wanted anything in my life. It didn't matter who delivered the fireworks, only that it was soon.

But the descendants like to take their time, and drag out the divine torture for as long as possible.

Dear god.

I might die in their arms.

It was at their mercy, and yet they only seemed to care about how they were making me feel. Neither was greedy nor combative, but they worked together to bring me right to the brink of desire. The release was right there. I bit down on my lip, my back arching forward when something fluttered over my arm. It happened again, soft and silky, pulling me away from the edge I so desperately sought. I was breathless, annoyed, and aroused to the point of no longer being held responsible for what I did next. My eyes slowly peeled open, and I gasped.

Obsidian butterflies swirled around the room in a stunning dance. Their velvety wings beat gracefully through the air, circling around the three of us. Our little intruders had seized the attention of Jase and Issik as well, but from the way their bodies had hardened against me, they weren't as infatuated as I was by them.

My head fell back as I followed their elegant forms. "They're beautiful."

Issik's fingers dug into my hips. "They're deadly," he informed me.

Exhaling, I turned my gaze to Jase in front of me. "Of course they are," I mumbled.

Issik picked me up like I weighed twenty pounds, and positioned me behind both of their massive bodies. "Don't touch them. Keep them away from your face."

I stared at his back, when all I really wanted to do was watch the mesmerizing butterflies frolic in the room. It was hard to imagine a creature I had spent summers chasing was harmful in another world.

The fierceness on Jase's expression just about stopped my heart. "The nightflies whisper commands into the ear of their prey, and the victim is powerless to do anything but obey."

"Mind control?" I shrieked. "But they're so small."

Issik nodded, never taking his laser focus off the little creatures. "They are born of a dark magic that doesn't exist in the Veil."

"She never gives up with her shenanigans, does she?" I retorted.

Issik scowled. "For almost a hundred years, she has tormented us with her tricks."

I swallowed hard, moistening my lips. "How are you not all insane?"

"Who says we aren't?" Jase countered with mischief in his eyes. He couldn't possibly be enjoying this.

But I supposed we all were a bit nutty at times. What we had been doing was incomparably the zaniest thing I'd ever done.

Jase twisted his head to the side so he could see me with one eye. "This is a great opportunity for you. Put them to sleep."

"No," Issik replied, rejecting the idea. "We're not putting her at risk. If something went wrong—"

My hand landed on his shoulder. "You don't think I can do it?" The urge to prove myself rose up strongly inside me. Issik had a right to be concerned. If I screwed up, I could potentially put myself in serious danger, and still, I wanted to do it.

I was tired of being useless.

A spark of willpower and confidence infused my blood. I blamed it on the descendants' kisses. They could make even the weakest of humans feel formidable.

Issik looked over his shoulder, careful to keep his gaze

directly on me. "This has nothing to do with my belief in you."

"Good, then it's settled." Before I could change my mind, I stepped out from Issik's shadow.

"Son of a bitch," he swore.

But I already had my mouth open, blowing a stream of purple mist into the air above my head. Issik and Jase made the smart decision to stay behind me and not try to stop me. The fluttering, mind-control devils went berserk at first, flying in the air like they were tripping on acid. Then as the effects of tranquility took hold, the assholes dropped to the ground one by one.

I spun around and grinned, dusting off my hands. "Easy peasy." That badass feeling returned, and this time, it stayed with me. I wasn't helpless, and I needed to remember I had power of my own.

"Great. Do you know what you've done?" Issik accused Jase. "She is going to be putting herself in twice as much danger now that she thinks she can zap everything to sleep. What happens when they wake up?"

Oh, snap. I hadn't thought about that. "Can't we have Zade burn them?" I asked. Surely, they couldn't wake up if they were ashes.

Issik swung his frosty gaze to me. "We could if he was here. Who knows when they will be back. We can't take that chance. There's no choice but to get rid of them before the nightflies shake off the effects of tranquility."

Jase nodded in agreement, scratching a hand over his chin. "They might be small, but they are also resilient, even to my power. We might have an hour, most likely less."

I liked it better when I was feeling ultracool. "Okay, so what's the plan? You have one, right?"

Jase grinned. "I always have a plan."

"Gather the nightflies," Jase barked. "But don't let the powder from their wings touch you. We'll take them into the kitchen and cook them."

My nose scrunched up. "That's morbid and gross."

Jase lifted a single brow. "You got a better idea?"

"Not really. It's just we eat there."

"Speaking of food, I'm starving. The kitchen works for me." Issik didn't seem to share my disgust.

Rolling up my sleeves, I stared at Issik like he'd grown a second set of balls. "Oh, my god. How can you think about eating right now?"

Issik shrugged. "High metabolism."

"You think Alice is going to let us roast these in her kitchen?"

Jase slipped off his shirt and ripped it in half. "Once she knows what they are, she'll insist."

Ooookay. "What's with the hulk move? You're not expecting me to walk around the castle shirtless too, are you?"

He handed me half of his torn shirt. "The only people who get to see you naked is us. Tie this over your hand."

I did as he instructed, securing the fabric over my fingers in a makeshift glove to act as a barrier against the nightflies. Jase wrapped the other cloth over his hand, and together the two of us gathered the dark and deadly butterflies scattered around the floor. Issik had removed his shirt as well, holding it out like a hammock for us to put the nightflies in, and transport them to the kitchen.

It took a few minutes, and then we were on our way down the hall. The castle was quiet with Kieran and Zade gone. Viperus Keep didn't have the staff or the number of girls that Wakeland castle had, or maybe they did a better job at being discreet.

The kitchen was empty when the three of us arrived. Issik set the bundle of nightflies on the stove, and snatched a roll from a basket, tearing off a hunk with his teeth.

My hip leaned against the counter, as I shook my head. "I don't know how you can eat."

Taking another bite, he worked his way through the kitchen, opening a cabinet. "The body needs fuel, and so do you. Sit down. I'll make you something."

"I'm not hungry," I replied without looking at him. I was too busy watching Jase light the fire on the stove, and drop the nightflies into the flames.

"Olivia. Sit." Issik raised his voice, putting a chill into it.

I snapped to attention, weaving around the counter to the table. "When did you become so pushy?" I grumbled.

He pulled some cans off of the shelves. "The moment your health is at risk."

"Sometimes I think you guys care too much," I stated, sinking into a chair and letting my shoulders relax. It had been a stressful day. My body was sore and achy. I needed a hot shower, but I indulged Issik, knowing his heart was in the right place. Plus, I was interested to see what the Ice Prince could whip up for me.

Jase finished incinerating the nightflies, and I tried to ignore the smell of charred wings that lingered in the air.

The foul deed was done. Tianna's little plan had been foiled. The sounds of Issik cooking in the kitchen relaxed me. Closing my eyes, I rested my head on the back of my chair, and kicked my feet up on the chair across from me. The one beside me scraped over the floor, and Jase's scent tickled my nose.

The warmth of the stove sent me into a stupor, and I might have dozed off for a little bit, because when I came to, the kitchen no longer smelled like putrid, burning insects, but of savory rich flavors. Butter. Herbs. Garlic. A mountain of pasta sat in the center of the table, next to a platter of chicken in a white sauce.

Zade, Issik, Jase, and Kieran were all sitting around the table. My gaze scanned over both Zade and Kieran. I sighed in relief, happy to have them back. They appeared to be fine, but starved. No run-ins with the witch. They each had a plate of food in front of them.

"You're back," I greeted still groggy, stretching out my stiff arms.

Kieran offered me a lopsided grin. "And you're just in time for dinner."

I missed hearing his slight Irish accent. They might have been gone for the day, but to me, it had been too long. I felt incomplete without being surrounded by the four of them, and sitting here at the table, my soul soared; I was whole.

"I'm famished."

Issik made a gruff sound in the back of his throat, and I grinned at him. Who knew the Ice Prince was a chef?

I listened to the others relay what had happened during the day as I stuffed myself. Jase told Zade and

Kieran about the nightflies, which earned me a pair of dark scowls. Zade informed us how their trip had turned up nothing on the Star of Poison. Sitting at the dinner table, discussing our day, made it feel like we were a family. I wanted a hundred—no a thousand—more nights like this. I wanted to be their family, and I needed them to be mine.

Was it conventional? No. But it didn't matter. Not to me. How they made me feel was what mattered most.

"I can't believe Olivia took out a nest of nightflies. How the hell do I miss all the good shit around here and this is my house?" Kieran complained.

"I'm proud of you," Jase confessed, ruffling my hair.

My heart swelled.

Jase's soft snore filled my ears. I didn't understand how these descendants were able to fall asleep so quickly. Turning on my side to face the slightly ajar window, I watched the moon's rays filter through the curtains, casting a pale light upon my face. A cool breeze caressed my skin.

I finally slept and dreamed. Regardless of how I fought against the invasion into my mind, Tianna always found a way.

In the dreams, the Star of Poison burned like a furnace in my hand, and green toxins spilled from the stone. I wasn't alone. A black mass withered the ground, scorching it with darkness.

The dream shifted. I was cradling Kieran's lifeless

body in my arms. The trees surrounding us wept with sadness, for the heart of their kingdom was dead. No matter how hard I cried, begged, or wished, nothing would bring the dragon shifter back.

My grief consumed me.

It had been days since we'd seen the sun. My face turned upward, soaking up the warm rays as they bathed my face. What I wouldn't give for a bathing suit, a bottle of Hawaiian Tropic suntan lotion, and a fruity drink with a pink umbrella. A perfect day lying out on the beach, the golden sun tanning my skin, and not a care in the world.

No curse. No deadlines. No impending deaths. That's what I wanted.

Lost in my fantasy, I twirled the charm hanging around my neck, strolling the grounds outside the castle. The pendant glinted under the sun, casting a ray of light out in front of me like a flashlight.

What the hell?

Looking down, I lifted the gold charm in my hand and watched in wonder as the light moved with my movements. Holy crap. This had to mean something, didn't it?

Like a kid with a new toy, I twisted and turned the circular charm in my fingers, watching as the beam bounced off everything it touched. It ran up the castle, tracing the winding stone snake, but as it got to the top, an unexpected flash of emerald joined the ray of light.

What is that?

My hand tilted the charm left and right, trying to reproduce that glint of green.

There! Inside the snake's eye cavity glimmered what I would have bet my left ovary was a gemstone—the gemstone.

I gulped. Why? Why did it have to be the creepy snake's eye? It had been right over our heads this whole time. How had we not seen it before? Other than the fact it was six stories high, and a vital part of a stone snake statue that twined around the main tower.

But I knew deep in my bones that nestled into Viperus's mascot's eyeball was the Star of Poison. I had found it, but getting it was altogether a different obstacle. Obtaining the Star of Tranquility had only involved holding my breath, and diving into the lake, but this was trickier. Still, it wasn't going to stop me.

Shielding my eyes from the sun with my hand, I stared up at the intimidating statue. Vines weaved around the castle like rungs on a ladder. I glared at the long journey ahead of me. The moment I grabbed the first strand of ivy, I knew this was going to end badly.

Me? Scale a castle?

Why would I even consider doing such a thing? The old Olivia wouldn't have contemplated it for two seconds. The old Olivia would have checked the new Olivia into a mental hospital. The old Olivia wouldn't have fallen for four dragons who had begun to mean everything to her.

She also never would have talked about herself in the third person.

Before I could change my mind, I started ascending the castle. I was about six feet off the ground when a voice sounded behind me. "What the hell are you doing?"

My head whipped over my shoulder to stare down at Kieran, who had his arms crossed over his chest. "Climbing the snake," I hollered down, doing my best to keep my grip secure. The last thing I needed was to tumble to my death.

"I can see that. But why?"

My arms were already tired—a bad sign. "I found the Star of Poison," I announced. A triumphant grin split my face. In my excitement, my right fingers loosened, and I slipped a few inches down the side of the castle, losing some of my progress.

"Get down here before you hurt yourself," he growled at me.

"Did you hear what I said?"

"Olivia, now!" he boomed.

"Geez. Keep your boxers on. You really know how to take the *f* out of fun."

"Are you telling me you're having fun?" he challenged me.

Good point. "I hate you," I replied as I carefully made my way back to flat ground.

Kieran plucked me off the vine when I was within reach, placing me safely on my feet, but his hands stayed at my waist, anchoring me to him. "No one knows more than I how much you don't hate me."

My worry of falling vanished. "Rub it in, why don't you?"

Kieran turned me around. "Why didn't you ask one of us to take you to the top, instead of trying to scale a castle?"

Duh. I had four dragons who could flippin' fly. "I got so excited that I didn't think about it."

"Clearly," he chuckled.

"Soooo…" I drew out the word. "What are you waiting for? Let's get the stone before you-know-who decides to show up, and rain on my freaking parade."

"Have I told you how strange you are today?" he asked, sounding both amused, and exasperated all at once.

I rolled my eyes. "Says the guy who is about to shift into an emerald dragon, and spits poison."

Kieran winked. "Valid point. I think that's why we like you so much."

"Oh, I thought it was because I'm a blonde."

"There's that too." Kieran grabbed the hem of his shirt and lifted it over his head. "Do you mind holding these?" he asked as he wiggled out of his jeans.

My eyes were glued to his abs, and it took me a moment to process what he had asked. Then I noticed the pile of clothes in his hands. "Let's be real. You did that on purpose so I would drool over your naked body."

Wickedness sparkled in his expression, as he dropped his clothes, and lifted his thumb to brush the side of my lip. "Here, let me get that for you."

I smacked at his hand. "Stop flirting with me and do your thing already. We're wasting time." I couldn't believe he was teasing me.

Where was his elation at finding the stone? This was what we'd spent the last few weeks searching for frantically. I wanted an *Olivia, you're a genius* or some other type of accolade. My gaze narrowed as I glared at Kieran and realized something. He wasn't taking me seriously. Bastard.

"You don't believe me."

"I never said that," he quickly replied, seeing my brows draw together.

I let out a loud huff. "For the love of dragon eggs, shift so I can prove to you that I'm not kidding." And so I was no longer subjected to the view of his gorgeous body. Ten more seconds and I might have forgotten what I was supposed to be doing.

He gave a little bow as if he was at my service, and his silver lip ring shone under the brilliant sunbeams. "As you wish."

With a roll of his neck, his limbs stretched. His skin became green as scales formed over his body. The transformation from man to dragon was a seamless process, but I always felt this tingle of magic tremble in the air, and I couldn't help but be in awe each time. How a man could possibly become such a breathtaking and ferocious creature was beyond my comprehension.

I waited until Kieran shook out the shift and settled into his dragon form. He eventually brought his head and long body to the ground, allowing me to climb aboard his back. His wings spread wide as he rose up to his full height and kicked off the grassy ground, causing my hair to blow back off my face. The flapping of his wings whooshed in the air as we went upward.

We circled around the castle once before approaching the head of the stone snake. My anxiety kicked up a notch inside my chest. Kieran had gotten me up the six stories, but I still had to manage to get myself onto the head of the snake.

"Do you think you can climb onto the roof without killing yourself?" Kieran asked. There was no mistaking the worry in his voice.

"Definitely," I replied with as much enthusiasm as I would have had eating a plate of alfalfa sprouts.

"Fuck me. This is a horrible plan. You're going to fall. I should have gotten one of the others to spot you."

"Thanks for the boost of confidence," I grumbled as I swung one leg around to meet the other. Kieran in dragon form was too large to land on the roof. "Maybe I could use your tail as a slide." The comment was supposed to be to myself as I thought out loud, and tried to gauge my success rate of various options.

"No!" Kieran stated flatly. *"You might go too fast."*

My right fingers stretched out for the roof. "Can you get me any closer?"

He was all business, reminding me of Jase. *"What do you think I'm doing?"*

Okay, new plan. I flipped my leg back over, and scooted up to his neck. I threw my arms around him. "Fly to the head of the snake. I'm going to reach out and grab it."

"I should have strapped you on," he snarled, but he used his expansive wings to turn us so we faced the castle head-on.

While he positioned himself, I drew my feet up, and

with care and wobbly knees, I began to stand up, keeping my arms secured around his neck. Once he was close enough for me to reach out, I leaned my whole body up against his long, thick neck, releasing one hand as the other clutched Kieran like he was my lifeline. And in a way, he was.

Anticipation trickled down to my toes. This was it. The moment we'd been waiting weeks for, ever since I'd found the first star. Being so close to our goal felt surreal —almost like one of Tianna's nightmares. My fingers grazed the stone, and I nearly jumped for joy. Wrong move. A gust of wind blew, smacking of magic, and it jostled Kieran, which then in turn made me lose my balance. I scrambled to get both my arms around Kieran or plummet like a ragdoll to my death.

"Olivia!" his voice yelled in my head.

I winced. "Geez. Not so loud."

"You're okay," he breathed in relief, shooting out a puff of poison.

"Yeah, but watch the toxic stuff. I don't want you to kill me before I get the star."

"Sorry, I lost it for a second when I thought you were going to fall."

"Me too. Quick, get me back over there before the bitch decides to grace us with her crazy presence."

"I think you might be the crazy one."

It was entirely possible, but I was willing to do anything to save the descendants, even tackle my fear of heights, and snakes at the same time.

Resituating myself, we went through the drill again— this time without hesitation. My fingers went into the hollow cavity of the snake's eye, and wrapped around the cool green stone. The very second I had a grip on it I yanked my hand back. It should have been a moment of celebration, but like most things in the Veil, nothing was as simple as it seemed.

A trail of green smoke exuded from the Star of Poison, climbing over my fingers, down my arm, and into my face. It cooled my skin—not like Issik did, but it dropped my body temperature nonetheless. Taking me by surprise, I inhaled, sucking up the smoke into my lungs.

Crap.

That was bad. Wasn't it?

It was called the Star of Poison, so the green mist had to have been poison. Right?

I guess I was about to find out.

Lucky me.

The urge to throw the glowing emerald crystal clutched in my hand was strong, but I held on, knowing that without it the dragons would never survive. My arms looped around Kieran's neck for stability as the poison in my nostrils worked its way through my body and settled around my organs. A jolt of energy slammed into me as soon as I had both hands around Kieran's neck. He must have felt it too.

"What the—" Kieran's head turned to the side, and I watched in shock as a milky film covered his bright green eyes. His wings went slack in the air and his body limp.

Oh, hell no.

This wasn't happening. Not again.

Like an airplane falling from the sky, gravity pulled the

weight of his body toward the ground. "Kieran!" I screamed.

Only feet away from slamming into the ground, he activated his wings, pulling us back up into the sky. *"What the hell just happened?"*

"You tell me. You're the one who became paralyzed mid-flight."

"I lost control... of everything. My dragon. My ability. Myself. It all vanished until you called my name."

"It was the stone," I answered with confidence.

After circling once in the sky, Kieran flew us steadily toward the front of the castle. My legs clung to his body, and I gripped the stone tightly in one hand. I didn't allow myself to think about what was happening inside me. All that mattered was I had the stone.

I could sense Kieran's rush of joy as he realized we had finally found the stone, and it made me smile. Kieran landed in the courtyard on a soft patch of vibrant grass. The tingles of his shift from dragon to man danced in the air the moment my feet touched the ground.

I could barely contain myself, waiting for him to shake off the last remnants of his dragon. Not even his nakedness distracted me. "Do you feel any different? Have your shackles to the isles been removed?" I held my breath, waiting for Kieran to answer.

He had one leg in his pair of jeans and was wiggling the other in. The wait for him to pull them over his hips was torment. I was dying to know if it had worked as it did for Jase. Leaving his pants unzipped and unbuttoned, Kieran flipped his wrists over, front to back, staring at them. For whatever reason, the magic Tianna had chained them with was invisible to my eyes—all human eyes actually.

I started to tap my right foot as I waited for him to respond. "Hello? Did you forget about me?"

Kieran finally lifted his head, a smile playing on his lips. Suddenly, I was in his arms and my feet were dangling off the ground. "You did it. I can't believe it, Blondie." Then he was kissing me breathless. "God, I love you."

With my arms twined around his neck, I stared at him with stars in my eyes. Had that been a flippant comment? Like "Oh, my god, you saved my life, and I love you for it"? Or was he actually professing his love for me? I shocked myself by really wanting Kieran to sincerely love me—not like a friend or a girl who saved his life.

I wanted the dragon to be *in* love with me.

Holy shit.

I wanted them all to be *in* love with me because it became crystal clear… I was in love with all four of them.

My breathing became labored.

Someone save me from myself. How could I possibly be in love with four very different guys? It wasn't just their dragon forms that set them apart; each one was unique in the same way their abilities were unique. I'd become just like the other women on the isles. I no longer wanted to be saved or rescued from the Veil. I wanted to attach myself more and more to the dragons who ruled these lands.

I stared into Kieran's expectant, happy face. "We should find the others," I replied, wanting to hit my head on the side of the castle. Why hadn't I told him how I felt? Why hadn't I said, "I love you too"?

Because everyone you've ever loved has left you.

Being the key to the dragons' survival didn't mean I wasn't damaged inside. Clearly, I was. The battle was far from over, and I might still lose those I held dear to my heart. Tianna could still win and take the descendants from me.

Then what?

I'd be left alone with a broken heart.

Again.

That was something I could not live through another time. Never again.

I had to protect myself, guard my heart, at least until the curse was fully broken. Then I could bare my soul, and I'd be free to tell them how I felt. I hoped when the time came, they wouldn't force me to choose between them. I couldn't. I wouldn't. But I would respect their decision. They meant that much to me. I would take them however I could get them. Not being a part of their life wasn't an option, regardless of how much their rejection might sting.

Kieran had yet to put me down on my feet. He pressed a quick, hard kiss on my lips as he walked us into the castle. I could do nothing but hold on and kiss him back with as much emotion as I could muster.

"What's going on?" A voice interrupted our bonding moment. It was Jase.

Elation tingled down my spine, and my cheeks flushed. When both of my feet touched the ground, I lifted my hand and opened my palm, showing him the vibrant Star of Poison. It pulsed with life.

Jase's eyes left my face, glanced at my hand, and then grew large. "You found it. How?"

I shrugged. "With this."

Using my other hand, I touched the pendant hanging around my neck. "It was the light that led me to the stone, just like she said it would." *She* being the woman in white. I had yet to figure out who the women were that kept appearing to me, but without their help, I never would have been able to locate either of the stars. These ghosts wanted to save my dragons as much as I did. I felt sure of it.

Jase's gaze zeroed in on Kieran's wrists. "They're gone. Just like mine."

Kieran grinned, holding up his arms and twisting his hands left and right. "No more magical shackles."

Running his fingers through his hair, Jase's dimples appeared, his face beaming. "I can't believe it. We might actually do this."

"Do what?" Issik asked as he exited the great room. His muscular form was followed by Zade's.

"Break the curse," Kieran supplied. He held out his hand, and I gladly turned the Star of Poison over to its rightful heir. He held it up between his thumb and index finger for the others to see. "Olivia found the star."

"No shit," Zade cursed in wonder.

Issik was studying me. It was hard to read his expression, but even though I thought he would have been happy, he didn't look pleased. "Are you okay?"

"I-I think so," I stammered, telling myself not to worry

about the burning in my chest. Most likely it would go away, or so I hoped.

He didn't believe me and had to check me out for himself. Cool fingers pressed against my chin as he examined my face. "The last time you touched a stone, you absorbed its powers."

I nibbled on my lower lip. "Uh, well, there was this green mist, and I sort of inhaled it."

"You did what?" Kieran, Zade, and Jase thundered. Issik was the only one who didn't say anything, but he shook his head.

"It wasn't like I planned on gulping down some poison. It just happened, and that was minutes ago. I'm still alive, so… no harm done."

I mean, did I feel different? Yes, but that was to be expected after swallowing a mystical mist. And although I didn't want to believe I now had another dragon breath swimming around inside me, the logic of it was I probably did, which meant I also had the burden of figuring out how to control it.

Jase snorted. "At this rate, you're going to be quite the formidable little human if you keep absorbing the stars. Tianna is going to want to get her hands on you for sure."

"We need to be ready," Kieran instructed, catching the eyes of the others. The room sobered quickly at the mention of the witch. "There's no telling when she will strike next, but it will be soon. She will have felt the crack in her spell."

None of us knew that "soon" was just minutes away.

"We will be ready for her," Zade vowed, puffing out his chest. His shirt stretched taut over his flexed muscles, making them visible through the thin cotton. "Star by star, we'll chip away at this curse."

I didn't want to be the one to bring up the obvious, but it had to be said. "What about your waning powers? Should you guys really be fighting a witch?"

It was as if I'd slapped each of the descendants across the face. They all wore shocked, how-dare-you expressions. The descendants considered themselves fierce warriors who could take on any foe, no matter what size or how strong—male, female, witch, wraith. Weakness was not an option. I commended them for their bravery and believed in their abilities, but it didn't change the fact that I worried about something happening to them. Too many times we'd stared death in the face.

The four dragons looked grim as we walked into the main hall. "Olivia, we have little choice. It isn't just about our survival. The entire isles are depending on us to keep them safe," Jase reminded.

Kieran closed his fist over the Star of Poison. "We will fight until we take our last dragon's breath. This is our responsibility as the last royal blood of our kind. We must stand against her."

"Even at the cost of your own life?" I argued. "Wouldn't that defeat the purpose of trying to save the dragons from extinction?"

Issik's face softened, losing some of the harshness that had materialized at the first mention of Tianna. "You care for us. We care for you as well, and understand the graveness of our situation. If anything ever happened to you—"

"What Issik is trying to say is we'd die to protect you, no matter the cost," Kieran finished.

I swallowed back a swell of emotion. They would risk the existence of dragons—of the Veil Isles—to keep me alive. I didn't feel worthy of such devotion, and what I didn't say was I was willing to die to save them too. Ironic.

Who would die first?

Because death was imminent, wasn't it?

Was it possible, was there even a slim chance, that all five of us would live to see another year?

A shiver of foreboding scampered down my neck, causing the hairs to stand up. I suddenly felt as if Issik was hugging me in the center of a wintery blizzard. "You should probably put that somewhere safe."

I indicated the stone clutched in Kieran's large hand. A piece of me wanted to hold it again. Something about the crystal called to me. I wanted to keep it close, tuck it under my pillow, but it wasn't a good idea. Distance, that's what I needed. Taking my advice, Kieran went to safeguard the star someplace secure, and hopefully magic proof—if such a place existed.

Needing a few minutes to get my wacky emotions under control, I started to walk out of the great hall, toward the stairs.

"Where are you going?" Issik demanded, blocking off my path like a giant boulder.

I had to think quickly. They wouldn't voluntarily let me out of their sight. "To change. These clothes reek of poison."

The ice prince lifted his brows. "Is that so?"

"Yeees?" I replied, looking guilty as hell. Why was it so hard to lie to them?

"Olivia." His voice had dropped below freezing.

"Issik," I rumbled back, rolling my eyes. "I'll be five minutes. I'm in the castle with four dragons. How dangerous can that be?"

"Be quick. I want us to stick together tonight." Issik stepped out of the way.

I strutted down the hallway, allowing myself a few minutes of solitude. The castle was deathly quiet, which I took as a bad omen. Nothing good ever followed a silence so complete. Nudging the door to my room open with my foot, I peeked inside. It was just as I'd left it. Canopy bed, wicker dresser, clothes on the floor—nothing amiss.

It didn't take me long to change into something more appropriate for running and kicking ass. Both were probably in my future. At the last second, before I headed back downstairs to join the descendants, I grabbed the dagger

Jase had given me, and tucked it into my boot. It couldn't hurt to be armed. Feeling more confident, I shut the door to my room and turned the corner.

Fear slapped me in the face, and the feeling was followed by the hissing of a snake—correction, multiple snakes. I knew that sound was bad news. It was my nightmares come to life.

I shuddered, sucking in a fortifying breath. *Don't turn around. Don't turn around. Pretend you didn't hear anything.* If only I could. Willing it away wasn't going to make what I was certain was coming my way any less real. My chest heaved as I took a breath and spun.

Holy dragon balls.

My head tilted to the side, transfixed by the figure headed toward me. "Is that... Medusa?" I mumbled to myself.

A woman stood in the center of the hallway leading into the great hall. I couldn't tell what color her hair was due to the numerous snakes twining around her neck and body. They slithered up her legs, wrapping around her waist and into her hair.

I wanted to puke.

Or faint.

Most definitely, I wanted to scream.

The red silky gown she wore clung to her like a second skin, moving fluidly as she swayed toward me. My feet backed up with each step she took forward, and yet, she somehow gained ground on me—the magic of a witch.

I was afraid. It helped to admit it and accept it. This wasn't the first, nor would it be the last time I'd be shaking in my boots because of our fight with Tianna.

And regardless of how scared I felt, I was determined to not give up.

Not now.

Not until the last second before the summer solstice.

The warmth in the hallway was eaten away by Tianna's presence. She might have draped herself in snakes and slapped on a different dress, but the wickedness that lived inside her was the same. Clouds of mist crawled along the wooden floors, and up the veins of ivy clinging to the ceiling.

"If you came for the stone, I don't have it." I was shocked to shit that my voice hadn't quivered.

"But you did find it, didn't you, dear? I felt the power of the stone leave its vessel, and attach itself to something." Tianna poked me in the heart. "I'm guessing that something is you."

"Nope. Not this time," I lied, keeping my chin firm.

"You're not a very good liar, Olivia."

"And you're a bit—"

Tianna placed her index finger and thumb around my lips. Then she pinched them shut, cutting off my impulsive response. I couldn't help myself around her. She brought out the demon inside me. I wanted to wrestle her to the ground, and strangle her with one of her disgusting pet snakes. The witch clucked her tongue at me, while I shot daggers of pure hatred tinged with a healthy dose of fear in her direction.

"Someone needs to learn to hold her tongue when speaking to her elders." One of her snakes agreed. It lunged forward at my face, hissing in anger. Its forked tongue tasted the air around my cheek, making me cringe in revulsion.

With my mouth clamped shut by her slim fingers, the words I attempted to throw at her came out in a muffled shrill.

"Cat got your tongue?" She laughed like it was the funniest line in the world. "Maybe this will help." She released my pinched lips.

I was two seconds away from spitting in her face. "What is with you and the reptiles? Couldn't you enlist some Care Bears to do your dirty deeds?"

"I'm going to assume that is some kind of insult." She regarded me with distaste. "Enough of the cute banter. You and I have a show to put on." Her slim fingers reached for my hand.

I jerked my arm away from her. "I'm not going anywhere with you."

Tianna put her hand on my shoulders and twirled me around. "You don't have a choice. Now move it, sweet cheeks." She shoved me forward. "I need you to give a believable performance."

I didn't see how that would be a problem, considering the fear I felt was very real. Mentally bracing myself for the fight to come, I berated myself for not putting my hair up into a messy bun or ponytail. Strands of hair kept falling over my face, making it difficult to see where I was going, and for what I was about to do, I needed a clear view.

Tianna was at my back, and I was glad she couldn't see my scheming face. It was a stupid plan, but it was the only one I could come up with under duress. Tianna had another thing coming if she thought I would be a pawn in her quest to get the dragon stars.

Not happening, witch.

On a whim of courage, I whipped out the blade inside my boot and pivoted. The knife thrust into Tianna's chest. I took a step back, leaving the weapon embedded inside her. Why wasn't she bleeding? Not even black blood oozed out of her.

Tianna threw her head back and laughed. She made quite the scene to behold, standing in the dim corridor in a ball gown with a dagger shoved into her heart. She pulled out the blade from between her breasts and smiled.

"Was that supposed to hurt? I'll give you points for effort, but really, Olivia, I'm disappointed in your originality. You couldn't have possibly thought a mortal blade could hurt me." Another haunting laugh filled with superiority released from her lips, as she chucked the blade across the hall.

But that wasn't the only thing she tossed.

Her hand swung toward my face, and the witch backhanded me silly.

I flew down the hall, landing near the stairwell hard enough to knock me unconscious. I barely held on as black dots swirled behind my eyes.

One good thing had come out of being slapped sideways. Mortal weapons might not be able to kill Tianna, but magical knives were fair game. Now I just had to get my hands on one.

No problem, I thought—heavy on the sarcasm.

"Olivia?" a deep voice called.

My eyes flew to Tianna. "No!" My scream took me by surprise.

Before I realized it, I was scrambling down the stairs and toward the sound of Issik's voice. Desperation tore through me. I had to warn them. My feet were flying over the steps, and by the grace of God, I didn't trip once or fall flat on my face. Issik was waiting at the bottom of the stairs, and I hurled myself over the last few and landed in his arms.

"She's coming," I panted, my eyes large with fright.

Issik took off with me in his arms, and I cursed the curtain of blonde hair that fell over my face. He burst into the great hall. "She's here," Issik hissed, handing me off to Kieran, who was still shirtless. The muscles in his arms and chest tightened as he set me on my feet.

They got into warrior mode. A wall of descendants stood in front of me. "I-I stabbed Tianna," I announced. My words came out in short bursts while I bent over to catch my breath.

"You what!?" four voices roared. Fire blazed in their eyes as the descendants judged me for a moment.

I pressed a hand gently to my cheek, and flinched at the sharp stab of pain. "Then the bitch hit me."

Based on the strength of their outraged shouts, I thought for sure the roof was going to collapse on us. Never had I heard such a low rumble. The floor vibrated under me. The chandelier above my head rattled. The walls trembled.

Zade cracked his knuckles. "She dies."

The others all seemed to be in agreement, making similar grunts of approval. Jase shook his head at me, running a finger over my jaw to take a look at the side of my face. "You're lucky to be alive. Kieran, get her the hell out of here. We'll take care of Tianna."

"No, you can't!" I pleaded, choking on the last word. Knowing she would come for the stone was nothing compared to actually having her in the castle, but not being able to see what she would do to the descendants scared me even more.

"Go!" Jase yelled.

Kieran's arms wrapped around my waist, and he lifted me off the ground. I twisted and kicked, flailing in Kieran's arms. "Put me down," I hissed. Being removed from the chaos that was descending upon me, threw me into a panic.

"Not on your life."

Kieran remained tense as he bolted out of the great hall, his longs strides swallowing up the floor. He took us to the rear exit of the castle that led straight into the woods. Behind me, Tianna's voice echoed throughout the stone halls. I couldn't hear her words, but the high pitch of her voice, was followed by several profound male ones. This was the deadliest game of hide-and-seek I'd ever played. I wanted to quit, but that would mean the witch would win.

Never.

Kieran sprinted outside, and the sky was pregnant with dark clouds. Rain spat and sizzled on the ground, casting up a haze of smoke. As the storm gushed, the air carried the scent of upturned earth. Pine needles covered the ground like a spiky blanket, and a bolt of lightning painted the leaves in a cheerful glow of yellow. Trees swayed heavily from the howling winds, like a thousand tortured voices. It was fitting the sun had decided to hide behind the clouds, while a lunatic witch was hunting me. If there was ever a day for gloomy skies and traces of doom, that day was now.

As Kieran moved us deeper into the woods of Viperus, a roar thundered from above our heads. Jase's dragon was circling the castle, his scales glistening from the mist of rain pouring from the menacing clouds. They weren't normal storm clouds, for they twisted and formed into a beast that lunged at Jase—another of Tianna's wicked spells.

"She's in the woods," I told Kieran.

His expression was gaunt. "I know."

He hung a sharp left, zipping over the ground with a speed that made me dizzy. His eyes were glowing and scales papered over his chest and arms. Kieran was tapping into his dragon, giving him extra strength and speed. This partial transformation fascinated me; I hadn't known he could.

"We can't outrun her forever," I stated. My arms were clinging to his neck.

Ducking under a large branch, he pressed on forward. "I don't plan on it. We're almost there."

"Where?" I asked, wondering what he was up to now.

"You'll see."

Jase came sweeping down from the sky in his dragon form, and barreled straight into a cluster of trees off to our left. I could guess what his target was. The witch. She was close, practically breathing down our necks.

Kieran felt it too.

Tianna was never alone in her fights. The prissy witch didn't like to get her blood red nails dirty. Instead, she had her cursed underlings do the honors. *Squawk. Squawk.* And here came the goonies.

"I fucking hate griffins," I mumbled, my eyes lifting upward. Through the trees, a pair of those evil assholes was locked on Kieran and me.

Kieran dropped me to my feet and pressed his forehead to mine. "Whatever happens, whatever you hear or see, you're not to leave this spot. Do you understand?"

What was so special about this specific spot? Did it have a protection circle? Or a secret trapdoor?

Turned out it was a tree. Not waiting for me to swear I wouldn't do something reckless, Kieran shoved me into the hollow of the tree before spinning around to shift. His large wing came up, blocking the entrance and keeping me locked inside. Unable to help myself, I peeked through a small crack, needing to see what was going on, or sit in here going mad. Kieran roared, letting a mist of green poison exude from his mouth. It swirled around the griffins, who pawed at the ground, kicking up dirt. They were smart and held their breaths.

Huddled in the corner, I listened as the sounds of a battle echoed over Viperus. It was gut-wrenching—the claws, the roars, and the cries—but nothing was worse than not knowing what was happening. A reverberating silence ensued. My heartbeat hammered in my ears as I cautiously crawled to the opening of the trunk. My fingers gripped onto the edge of the bark. Extending my neck and tilting my head to the side, I went to take a peek, but someone else had the same idea.

A griffin's head popped inside the hole. It shrieked in my face, blowing my hair back and spitting goo into my eyes.

Disgusting.

I scuttled backward on my ass, wiping a hand over my eyes. The substance was thick and sticky like snot. It also temporarily blinded me—at least I prayed it wasn't permanent. I told myself not to panic, but this was one of those times my body didn't listen to my brain, and I was moments away from losing my shit. Blinking rapidly, I tried to wash away the film that blocked my vision, but it was to no avail. Fear clogged my throat. The griffin who had me trapped inside the tree trunk made a clucking noise, its beak brushing up against the side of my face. I froze, my heart jumping out of my chest.

Holy shit. It's going to peck me to death.

My hands flew out in front of me, warding off an attack I was sure would come.

Claws dug into my shoulders, ripping through my clothes. I cried out in pain as the nails pierced my flesh. The searing agony intensified when the griffin dragged me out of the hole. I dug my heels in, swinging my fists sightlessly. It was useless, but that didn't mean I would give in, never.

Opening my mouth, I tilted back my head and released a puff of tranquility. I could be aiming at anything, including one of my dragons, but one thing was certain, I hadn't hit the griffin holding me captive.

My feet were no longer on the ground. I couldn't believe what was happening. The griffin was hauling me off into the air. Where were the descendants? What had Tianna done to them?

Without me, the descendants would never find the last two stars.

They would perish.

The Veil would be destroyed by a witch, and all those who lived here would be enslaved, tortured, or worse.

No! No! Hell no!

Fucking great. I'd been kidnapped again. This time not by four incredibly sexy dragons, but by a witch with a vendetta.

To be Continued...

A NOTE FROM THE AUTHOR

Thank you so much for reading Absorbing Poison, Dragon Descendants, book 2.

I truly hope you have enjoyed reading it, if you have, please show your support by leaving a review. It only takes few moments, visit my Amazon Author page:

J.L. Weil
https://amzn.to/2OPz6J3

Olivia's and the descendants' journey continues in
Taming Fire, Dragon Descendants, book 3

For the latest news about new releases, sales, upcoming books, giveaways, and more join my news letter today!
http://www.jlweil.com/vip-readers

ABOUT THE AUTHOR

USA TODAY Bestselling author J.L. Weil lives in Illinois where she writes Teen & New Adult Paranormal Romances about spunky, smart mouth girls who always wind up in dire situations. For every sassy girl, there is an equally mouthwatering, overprotective guy. Of course, there is lots of kissing. And stuff.

An admitted addict to Love Pink clothes, raspberry mochas from Starbucks, and Jensen Ackles. She loves gushing about books and Supernatural with her readers. She is the author of the International Bestselling Raven & Divisa series.

Don't forget to follow her!

www.jlweil.com
www.facebook.com/jenniferlweil
www.twitter.com/JLWeil
www.instagram.com/jlweil

Made in the USA
Las Vegas, NV
07 December 2020